GHOST STORIES

CLIFFORD JAMES HAYES

www.hayesdesign.co.uk/books

OTHER BOOKS AVAILABLE:

The Complete Murkmyre Saga
The Idiot
Out of my Head
Ísklo - A Dragon Tale
Augustus, the Hairy Zummabeest
The Slug that Saved Christmas
The Easter Bunny Invasion
The Easter Bunny's Outer Space Adventure
The Easter Bunny's Undersea Adventure
Utterly Bonkers (with Phoenix Petit-Hayes)
Grandma Grunt
Grandad's Bottom
Horrid Horatia
Hairy Tales
Verity Fruitt and My Magic Gonk

For other titles available (printed, ebook and audiobook formats), do a search for 'Clifford James Hayes' on Amazon.

CUSTOMARY AUTHOR'S NOTE:

It may seem as if there are many, many shocking inaccuracies and punctuation niggles lurking within this book's waffle - however, these are entirely deliberate.

Well, that's my excuse - and I'm sticking to it.

GHOST STORIES

CLIFFORD JAMES HAYES

Written, designed and published by Clifford James Hayes

www.hayesdesign.co.uk

Copyright © Clifford James Hayes 2021

Ghost Stories, 2021 edition.

ENTER ...

Seven lost souls. Seven solitary figures from seven different walks of life making their way uncertainly across a bleak, mist-obscured landscape; a foggy miasma that obscures everything about them. Slowly but surely they are coming together, and will soon meet, but for now they each stumble on alone through this twilight realm.

Each is confused about a great many things; how they arrived in this strange and unforgiving land, where they have come from and indeed where they are going. Above, a sombre blanket of unbroken cloud prevents any light from the sun, moon, or stars - this twilight will give no clues to time of day or night. Distant thunder rattles, and ripples of electrical storm pass through the shroud above. There is no rustling of leaves in trees, for there are neither trees nor wind; there is no bird or animal call, for both are utterly absent.

The seven's feet trudge onward, the strangely powdered, ashen landscape absorbing all sound from their tread and the dank, cloying mist making each shiver with its touch.

Some are more sure-footed than others; take Mr Quentin D'Orsay for example. He's a tall, some would say *arrogant* Englishman who strides confidently onward, concealing the truth of his terror and confusion from himself if no-one else. Captain Martin Jeddoe is close by; a Roundhead soldier who unfortunately is almost petrified with superstition and fear. He stumbles with almost every step, looking about himself, clutching at the small cross around his neck and calling aloud in the hope that someone will hear.

Then there's a young musician, Mr Benton (who prefers to just go by the name Travis), sucking on a cigarette and digging his hands deeper into his denim jacket's pockets as he shivers from the dampness of his foggy surroundings. He's not *too* concerned; his optimistic outlook is he'll always end up somewhere eventually. He just wishes he could *remember* something, as traipsing across this dire landscape is just about all he *can* remember at the moment.

Just ahead of Travis is 'the bride' - Emmeline Digby. Her lace and silk dress cling to her skin, and are no match for the moisture in the air or the crumping ash on the ground beneath her feet, which kicks up when she walks and leaves her clothing a tint of sickly grey.

A young Indo-American lady - Jaya Balakrishnan - isn't far from her, who also struggles along with her outfit; in her case a hefty spacesuit. Soon she'll make Mrs Digby's acquaintance, and both, as you can perhaps understand, will initially show considerable alarm at one-another's appearance.

The two stragglers are Mr Zacchariah Blake, a mortician and former soldier, and finally a young lady from the tiny African nation of Xanbaru - who, like Travis, prefers to solely go by her forename Yatima. It's fair to say that Mr Blake, due to his profession and experiences in his life, may have a quicker understanding of their circumstances. He has already paid considerable attention to the grey ash on which they tread, and stopped momentarily to dig a little deeper, whereupon he uncovered a foundation of broken bones and teeth.

It's unclear how long each of the seven have walked over this misted plain, but the time eventually comes for them all to meet. Captain Jeddoe's calls are heard by Mr D'Orsay, who responds with the same. They close in on one another's voices, and, once they have met, go through a predictable list of questions until both realise that the other can give no clue to their predicament. They are, of course, curious in regards to the manner of speech and clothing of the other (and Mr D'Orsay, due to his nature, is extremely *suspicious*), but both say little about this; each has a companion, and for now that is all that matters.

They proceed to call out together, and soon Travis has joined their small party. The ritual of questions and quiet curiosity is of course repeated, and eventually the trio walk on.

While all the above is unfurling, a similar set of events are in motion close by. Mrs Digby hears the heavy footfall of Ms Balakrishnan's spaceboots when she is closer to her, and is at first somewhat terrified. The spacesuit silhouette that appears out of the mist elicits a shriek of alarm from Mrs Digby, as you might expect. All is soon mended when Ms Balakrishnan opens the visor of her helmet; she is not a creature from the mist, after all. The state of affairs makes instant friends of Mrs Digby and Ms Balakrishnan, and they walk on as a duo. Then, within five minutes or so (if their environment allows us to measure time in this manner) they meet Mr D'Orsay and co., and the group is almost complete.

I mentioned a pair of stragglers earlier. Mr Blake decides to sit down and rest, to give his prosthetic leg a break from the discomfort it is causing. Yatima, perhaps as superstitious in temperament as Captain Jeddoe, is distracted by her fears and fails to see Mr Blake in the murk. She falls over him, and shouts in terror in her Wolof tongue. Mr Blake, having spent time in Xanbaru during his earlier career as a soldier, is able to placate her with the few words he knows of her language - though, like all the others, he has no recollection of anything before this nigh-endless trudge across the plain. Eventually, Yatima and Mr Blake also agree to go on together and converse in a mixture of French, Wolof and English until they have met the five others.

By chance or otherwise, their place of meeting was in front of a monumental pair of doors, that rose quite unexpectedly out of the mist. After a little deliberation, and with nothing else discernable in any direction, the seven decide to knock on them.

Although the doors are enormous in stature (and presumably very thick), the seven soon hear the tap and clack of shoes approaching from the opposite side.

Mr D'Orsay made to shout a message to the other side, but before he had chance to do so the doors began opening - to reveal a substantial and spacious room, devoid of all furnishings except for a large, circular sofa and a cocktail bar.

There was of course someone in the room waiting for them; a smartly-suited individual who quickly set about ushering the group of seven in and making them welcome.

"Please, please, *come in*," he began, courteously, "... sit down, do. Anyone care for a drink?" The host busied himself for a minute or two, settling people on the settee, flitting to and from the bar and passing around glasses of wine and spirits.

Cordial and friendly, he did his upmost to make his guests feel relaxed and at ease, and threw compliments and *bon mots* around the room like confetti; "Oh, Mr D'Orsay, that is a *smashing suit*; you really must tell me your tailor," and "Ms Balakrishnan, do let me take your space helmet; there's plenty of fresh air in *here*, you'll be pleased to know."

"You seem to know all *our* names," Ms Balakrishnan replied warily. "Does our *host* have a name - Mr ... ?"

"*Charon* is fine," the host replied genially, "though it's fair to say I've had plenty of other names over the years."

"And what is it you *do*, Mr Charon?" enquired Mr D'Orsay, who decided to forego a single wine glass and head straight for the entire bottle. "It seems a ridiculously lonely place, being stuck out here in the middle of nowhere."

"*Nowhere indeed*," the host said quietly. "Let's just say I help lost souls find their way, Mr D'Orsay." He surveyed the whole ensemble, now they were settled. "... And you *are* all *lost*, aren't you?"

"I-I guess we all *are*," said Travis. "I mean, I don't know about anybody else, but so much of my memory's just ... *gone*. I don't know what this place is, nor how I ended up coming here." A hubbub of anxious 'nor I' and 'me too' responses filled the room.

"So where *are* we?" Jaya Balakrishnan asked, firmly.

"All in good time," Mr Charon said placatingly, "all in good time - though I've a feeling Mr Blake may have an idea or two already, due to his profession. Let's just call this 'the waiting room', and while we *are* waiting, I thought it might be nice if we all got to know one another better - after all, doesn't *everyone* have *a story* to tell? And seeing as all your memories are somewhat 'hazy' at the moment, I'll be more than happy to fill in the blanks. So ... whose tale shall we begin with?"

THE ANANSIE BOX

Yatima Achebe sighed as she glanced in her rear view mirror at the pair of rich Belgian tourists bouncing around on her 4x4's back seat. She'd spent a long, long day showing them the sights and sounds of Xanbaru and just wanted to go home.

She'd taken them on a dawn safari to see hyaenas and a pride of lions in the wild, followed by a visit to a traditional native Wolof village. After that, they'd spent a long afternoon boating around mangrove swamps, looking for crocodiles and admiring some of her tiny nation's flora and fauna of interest.

And that should have been that. Unfortunately, the tourists had just decided they had *other* plans for her.

"Take us to one of your *markets*, Mademoiselle Achebe," instructed Claude, the slick-haired boyfriend, over the growl of her jeep's engine as it rocked and shook its way over the uneven road. "Sylvie and I want to hunt for some bargains."

Yatima politely protested that it was getting late, and that better deals could be found the following day in the market in her *own* village, Diouf, where their hotel compound was. *Just give me a night to rest and get over the smell of your nasty aftershave, Claude, and I'll gladly take you there in the morning,* was what she *really* wanted to say to her passenger. *And please don't call me Mademoiselle Achebe,* she would also say - *Achebe was my good-for-nothing father's name. I'm just Yatima - always have been, always will.*

But Claude wouldn't have any of it, and mocked her for wanting to call it a night so early. "Oh, *come on*, Mademoiselle, what are we *paying* you for? I just saw the sign for Kaffrine back there; Ali the concierge at the hotel said they do great carvings and rugs in the market at Kaffrine."

Of course he'd say that, thought Yatima; *most of Ali's extended family are market-traders in Kaffrine.* Grinding her teeth, she took the next turn-off and took her guests on their unplanned market-grab.

Yatima shook her head as she saw her two tourists jump from the back of her open-top vehicle and skip off laughing toward the sights and sounds of the market. They would get *fleeced*, she knew - ripped off by sleazy merchants. Alternatively, they would get robbed - or worse. *Just remember your job,* she chastised herself, and headed off after them.

The keen-eyed locals *pounced* on the pair of naive Europeans as soon as they saw them. Children with cupped hands ran toward them begging for money and tugged at Sylvie's 'safari pants'. Upright, healthy-looking men grabbed sticks, brushes or whatever else they could find and became instant cripples - limping toward them both, emulating the children and wailing as loud as they could in their mock-impoverished despair.

Yatima had noticed that throughout the day Sylvie had developed an irritating habit of *whacking* at children with her fly-swatter, and she was employing this tactic here with considerable ferocity.

At this, Yatima felt half-tempted to jump back in the jeep and leave them to it ... but no, she had a job to do, as well as a payment to receive at the end of the day; which she'd only receive after their safe return to the hotel compound. Sighing, she caught up with her charges and, yelling obscenities in her Wolof tongue, quickly shooed away their assailants.

The market in Kaffrine was *really* nothing special, she thought, as they sauntered from shop to shop and stall to stall, but Claude and Sylvie seemed enchanted by what they referred to as its 'West-African charm'; its silks and spices, its vibrant colours and smells, its street food and carvings. They seemed *determined* to buy as much *old crap* as they could carry.

Once the vendors had spotted Yatima's Mazibor Hotel tour-guide clothing they used it as a means to open a conversation with their potential victims; "Ah, you stay at the Mazibor - you know my brother Ali, the concierge? I will give you *good* price."

Yatima rolled her eyes each time; she'd heard it all before a thousand times or more. And she knew Claude and Sylvie would be too dumb to even bother *haggling* with the sly traders; *anyone who sells anything to these two tonight will end up rich enough to shut up shop for three months* - which also meant less 'tip money' for *her* for at the end of the night.

Tip money was something she desperately needed; with her parents gone, it was up to her to keep on top of the bills at her tiny home just outside the hotel's compound - her useless older brother Moussa never contributed anything other than empty beer bottles.

Every night she'd look from her bedroom window at the sheer white walls of the Mazibor Hotel directly behind her house; sometimes it was inconceivable to her how there could be so much wealth and comfort on one side of that big white wall, while there was so much poverty and suffering on the other side. Still, she had a job there, which meant a foot in its door - just so long as she didn't mess things up the 'all-powerful' Ali the concierge.

Sylvie caught sight of a café near the market's centre and insisted they stop there for refreshments. Really, Yatima knew she just wanted to have a go on a hookah pipe in the hope it contained something 'herbal and medicinal'.

Getting them both whacked out of their faces on weed might not be a bad idea, she briefly thought to herself; *it'd make my life easier.* Yatima made to sit down with them, but an awkward moment arrived where it was clear she wasn't invited.

"It's okay, Yatima, said Claude, shiftily, "why don't you go and ... take a tour for twenty minutes? Gives us chance to soak up the atmosphere, in peace."

This was backed up by an icy stare from Sylvie.

There was that big white wall again.

"*Màa ngui lay nianal weurseuk,*" Yatima replied sarcastically, giving them a grimaced smile. *Good luck.* She would've warned them about pick-pockets and given them effective methods to use on begging children that *didn't* require a fly-swatter (shouting *May ma jaam!* always worked for *her*) - but to hell with them for treating her so coldly after all the places she'd taken them that day.

So take a tour she did. Or at least, she ambled off no more

than fifty yards or so, as she knew Sylvie would quickly start screaming at locals and they'd both probably need her again before long.

Yatima soon found herself outside a shop that declared itself to be an antique dealers. She knew all dealers were serviced by an army of workers knocking out fake replicas, and doubted this shop was any exception. At first glance it had the usual wares; Persian carpets, tribal mask carvings, faded flags, rusted retro junk, wooden chests and 'native' trinkets - but it was as good a place as any to go while her tourists had 'a bit of space'.

She looked back toward the cafe. In the distance, she could make out Sylvie amongst another gaggle of children. She had her fly-swatter out again. "May as well take a look," Yatima sniffed, ignoring the growing melee surrounding her wealthy Belgian couple, and headed inside.

The shop was one of the few in the market that was an actual *building*. Most of the others were stalls; a few drapes to keep out the worst of the afternoon sun and the dust when the winds kicked up, all held up by tent poles and the like. The shop was old, and *felt* old; certainly from colonial times, and Yatima liked the quaint tinkle of the brass bell as she pushed its door open and stepped inside.

There was an ancient, bent-up woman squatting in shadows behind the counter in the corner of the shop. She was swathed in layers of ragged shawls despite the muggy nocturnal heat, and a pair of beady, shining little eyes poked out from beneath a veil and bandage-like layers of head wear.

Apparently disinterested in Yatima, she watched an Arabic programme on a small black and white television set, the light from its flickering image dancing across her semi-concealed face. Yatima nodded to her but got no response.

She got the impression the old woman ran the place herself; there was no background chatter from younger generations through the exit to the back of the store, and to be frank the place needed a decent clean - there was dust and cobwebs *everywhere*. Apart from the staticy, subdued voices from the old TV the place was silent. Eerily so.

Regardless, Yatima smiled and hummed to herself as she browsed the old woman's wares - not having to deal with the childish whims of spoilt European tourists or run around after her lazy brother Moussa back home was a rare treat indeed. And it went without saying that it was nice to be without Ali the concierge breathing down her neck. He *loved* to play one tour-guide off against the other and, most probably because she'd never been impressed by his unsavoury attentions, it was always a struggle to get the better-paying tourists from him for herself.

Tourists. If only she could be one *herself*, she found her rambling mind saying. If only she could get away from the heat, and the dust, and the sand and the poverty - not to mention the civil wars that kept happening in Xanbaru every few years. To *actually* fly on a plane out of there - just to see something like *snow* once in her life! How wonderful that would be!

There was the constant need to *pander* to the tourists, and to bite your tongue at their ignorance, in the hope of a small tip at the end of each day - and then hope that Ali wouldn't find some spiteful reason to hold it back from her. Oh, it would be good to even get away from lazy Moussa, just for a while.

She realised she was repeating a mantra she rolled around in her head every night. *Just forget it*, Yatima. And be grateful for the tour-guide job.

Her eyes passed across the array of wall-mounted wood-carvings and picture frames, replica spears and drums. Her fears had been confirmed - this shop was just like all the rest; crammed with crudely-made junk, and displaying nothing 'antique' whatsoever - just 'Africanised' fayre to appeal to tourists with more money than sense.

Oh, well - at least it had all been a brief distraction. Realising she'd best go and rescue Sylvie before she got into some *serious* trouble with the locals, she turned to make toward the shop's front door. Yatima found herself stopping in her tracks, however, when the glint of a solitary object on a web and dust covered shelf inexplicably caught her attention.

From a distance it seemed to be nothing spectacular; just another drab, poorly carved wooden box, that was about the size of a small trinket chest - but eight tiny jewels on its lid *shimmered* in the old shop's sepia light as she moved toward it, and for some unfathomable reason she felt the compulsion to investigate further.

Standing in front of the box, she could see the gemstones more clearly - they were most probably coloured paste replicas, she told herself. They'd been fashioned into the woodcarved design on the box, and now she was up close to it she could see that together the gems acted as the eight glistening eyes of a spider.

The woodcarving had been shaped to suggest a fat spider's body on the lid, while its eight legs were engraved in such a way to look as if they were dangling down on to the sides of the box.

Almost like a claw, she shuddered to herself.

Bold stripes had been chiselled on to the spider's body, and had been hand-painted yellow and black - overall, these elements gave the effect of a large, stripy-bodied *orb-weaver*; the kind of large-bodied, spindly-legged creatures that hung on enormous webs between the branches of the baobab and mangrove trees.

Perhaps the most curious aspect of the box's design had been applied to one of its sides - the panel beneath the cluster of glittering eye-gems - for most of this had been smoothly carved away, to give the impression of a cavernous, gaping *mouth* between a pair of enormous carved fangs, with nothing visible but an impenetrable blackness inside the chiselled orifice, should you try to peer inside. Yatima then realised this mysterious little box had no obvious lid, drawers or other method of opening - it was merely a wooden block with a deep hole fashioned into one side - and she admitted to herself she failed to see its purpose.

"It's an *Anansie box*," a close, grating voice said suddenly, making Yatima half-jump. In her surprise, she looked down to see the ancient shop-keeper had silently appeared beside her. Now she was close, Yatima lost a breath in her shock at the old woman's features; beneath her veil, her skin looked dried and dessicated, like the tissue-thin skin of a corpse. She smelled that way too; dusty and stifling, and Yatima found it hard not to elicit a cough.

There was something *about* that veil, she noticed; it was so fine and wispy, and fluttered gently despite there being no breeze in the dry and dusty store; it was more like the gossamer silk of *cobwebs* than finely-crafted lace. And before she could stop herself, Yatima found herself asking with weak, suffocated words what an Anansie box *was*.

The old woman gave what sounded like a laugh, though it could just have easily been the sound of dry bones rubbing together. "Oh, *Yatima*, what do you *think* it is?"

Disturbed this crone knew her name, Yatima stammered and found herself unable to answer. Instead, she followed the old woman's lively little eyes, which were now *feasting* on the box in a most *ravenous* manner. Yatima followed her gaze, and looked on the box once more. The eight glittering jewel-eyes; the eight slender legs, coiled claw-like around the box's sides; the bloated, stripy body ... and the open black maw of a hideous mouth. And then, uncontrollably, Yatima found herself slowly raising her left hand and *placing it* within the sinister chasm.

In panic and confusion, she looked back at the old woman, who was gently nodding contentedly - a cracked smile playing on her lips. She was wringing her clutched hands together with nervous fingers playing over one another as if in eager anticipation, her fiery, glinting eyes in total focus on the box and the hand that was placed within it.

Yatima screamed in white hot pain as she felt something *bite down hard* on the back of her hand. The burning, *excruciating* pain of what felt like fangs *crunching* into the thin flesh of her hand travelled like lightning up her arm toward her thumping heart ... while a vision of a woman's face with *eight unblinking eyes* stared deeply into Yatima's own. And then all turned black.

She woke to find Claude, Sylvie and a gaggle of locals standing over her. She screamed again in recollection of what she'd experienced and immediately reached for her left hand, to strike away that infernal box and whatever hideous *thing* had been lurking inside of it, waiting to bite her. But there was nothing there. No bite marks, no box, no creature within, no gloating old woman. Yatima was no longer in the old shop, but lying on her back in the dirt and gravel of the street outside.

She made to get up suddenly, but found herself woozy and reeling when she tried to stand. As she staggered, Claude and a street vendor caught her and helped her to a low wall so she could sit down.

Sylvie asked her what happened, and memories of the old antique store and the box came flooding back. Despite all else that was happening, a part of Yatima laughed to see Sylvie still hadn't shaken off a group of persistently begging little children, who were seemingly making a game of their baiting of the agitated European lady.

"The shop!" Yatima suddenly called out. "That old *witch* and her Anansie box!" She immediately looked about herself, and saw the store just to her right - it was closed now, with louvred blinds shut in windows caked in dust and grime. The sign above it was faded and cracked by heat and sunlight - it looked as if it hadn't been open in years.

Yatima got up again, making *toward* the shop - Claude tried to stop her, but brushing him off she groggily pushed past the crowd of slack-jawed onlookers until she reached the front of the store, then pushed hard on its entrance with the palms of her hands. It was shut - flaking paint crumbled away as she pushed and pushed - but it wouldn't open.

"Who *owns* this shop?" she asked of the nearest local, who looked at this crazy woman blankly. She asked another, and another, until someone - a old Gambian fruit vendor from the nearest stall - came forward to answer.

"*Nobody* lives there, lady," he explained, "that old shop has been empty *for years*. See for yourself."

He walked toward the shop's front door, spat on his kaftan's sleeve and used its fabric to wipe away some of the grime from its window.

Once he'd finished, he beckoned Yatima to look through the smeared glass - though it was dark, she could make out bare floorboards illuminated by the market's lights outside, and bare walls at the back of the shop.

"You see?" asked the vendor. "Nobody live there now - it empty."

"But - but ... I was *in* that shop, just before," Yatima protested. "Moments ago. Somebody must have seen me, right? I-I walked in ... looked around, and then that old woman ..."

The fruit vendor paused in thought. "There *was* an old woman, who used to run that shop ... but *she went away*, lady. Or perhaps she die; it was *many years ago*. I was a *young man* when that place was open, and look at me now." He began to chuckle. "But you; I think you just hurt yourself, lady. Maybe you bang your head. I think you just need to rest."

It wasn't long before Yatima was heading back to the Mazibor Hotel in her 4x4, but as a rear passenger this time, with Sylvie's mound of market shopping beside her. Claude was at the wheel on his insistence, with Sylvie in the front seat beside him. He'd briefly asked around for a doctor in Kaffrine for Yatima, but as no-one was available, the on-site medical practitioner back at the hotel seemed a preferable option. Within forty-five minutes they'd returned to the hotel, and Claude called on Ali the concierge to get Yatima checked over.

For the sake of keeping up appearances with the hotel clients, Ali disguised his reluctance to assist Yatima and immediately sent her to see Fatou, the hotel's medic, as Claude demanded.

Once she'd assured them that she would be okay from now, Claude and Sylvie paid Ali for Yatima's tour-guide services and headed off to the hotel's all-night bar, with a promise to check in on her the following day some time. *Maybe those two aren't so bad after all*, Yatima found herself thinking, with a rueful smile, *though I still hate Claude's nasty aftershave.*

Once she was in Fatou's office, the big Ghanian medical practitioner gave Yatima the kind of routine examination I'm sure you're familiar with - checking her pulse, pupils, throat and so on.

Once this was all done and satisfactory to Fatou, Yatima asked her to check her left hand; to see if there was any evidence of anything like bite marks, or puncture wounds, or if there was any sign of poisoning. There was nothing to see on her hand, but Fatou quietly obliged, and took a blood sample for toxicity to be checked.

With it now being late at night Fatou doubted she'd have any emergencies to deal with in relation to the hotel's clientele - the morning was always worse, when cures for hangovers were always in demand - so she told Yatima she had plenty of time to hear the full story of why Ali the concierge had actually allowed one of his own tour-guides to use the hotel's medical facilities; it must be an interesting tale, she told her, as it had never happened before on *her* watch.

Yatima laughed at this; Ali's mean reputation extended far and wide, it seemed. She was reluctant to say anything at first; there was much to her experience that didn't make any sense. Smiling, Fatou wandered over to a cabinet and returned with two glass beakers and a bottle of brandy.

"For medicinal purposes, you understand," joked Fatou. "Now, come on, girl - tell me your story."

And so, over *three* glass beakers of brandy, Yatima told her everything. From the routine day of tour-guide duty for two *initially* irritating Belgian vacationers, to the tedious diversion to Kaffrine and Sylvie's fly-swatter. From the saunter around the market, to the old antique shop with the sinister old woman behind the counter, and finally to the Anansie box and the terrifying, mystifying things that followed.

"Anansie," mused Fatou aloud, "he's the spider trickster - you know the stories?"

"*Everybody* knows Anansie," replied Yatima. "My brother used to tell me the tales when I was a child. Story-telling's the only thing he was ever good at. But there was never anything *bad* about Anansie; he was always foolish in the stories, tricking around, turning life upside down for others."

Yatima shuddered, despite her comments. Snakes she didn't mind. Scorpions, even.

But spiders she *detested*.

She neglected to mention to Fatou that when she was little her brother also used to think it funny when he'd fetch big spiders into their bedroom and torment her with them.

"Hmm ... but there are *other* stories about spiders, you know," Fatou said. "Supernatural tales. And maybe they're not just stories."

They were both quiet for several moments, until Yatima broke the silence with an awkward laugh. "Oh, listen to the *woman of science* here! Talking about ghosts and evil things! You'll get me believing it all!"

Fatou laughed with her. "I'm sorry, girl, it sounds like I'm mocking. But we had *bad* stories, back home, back in the day - things that make no sense - and not all of them can be explained with science and the modern way of life. But you want to know what I think happened to *you*? Hallucination. Daydreaming. Having to pamper rich Europeans day after day after day. And then there's that lazy-ass brother of yours to deal with when you get home at night. You're *tired*, Yatima. And I'm going to tell Ali you need a few days off, *with pay*, whether he likes it or not. Now, you get yourself home."

Yatima made to protest about agitating Ali, but Fatou insisted. "Oh, don't worry about that trumped-up little concierge man; I used to nurse him for his mother when he was a baby. Maybe I'll threaten him with telling everybody how he used the potty until he was seven years old. *Dinala*

Gis-Waat Duyaga, Yatima, and leave everything to me."

And so Yatima got her few days off - *five*, in fact, as Fatou made good on her promise to threaten Ali with the potty story when he was initially resistant. Fatou even made sure he passed on the not-inconsiderable tip money from Claude and Sylvie.

Yatima rested well for the first couple of days - better than she had in a long while - even managing to sleep through her annoying brother Moussa's late night drinking and card-playing with his unsavoury friends.

She relaxed around the hotel during the day, enjoying a chilled couple of hours at the beach bar and even (naughtily) using the customers' swimming pool when she knew Ali was off-shift.

She bumped into Claude and Sylvie once, and thanked them again for their help and intervention. She wasn't surprised to see they'd already landed themselves a *new* tour-guide - oh, well; they'd be back in Belgium soon and she could fix herself up with a new set of tourists when she was back at work.

On her third day off, whilst washing the dirty glasses and plates Moussa had left from the night before, she noticed something on her left hand.

Two tiny red marks.

She froze in that moment. They were *precisely* where she'd felt the needle-like fangs bite into her in the old antique shop. Shaking, she went to touch them delicately with two fingers of her right hand, and flinched with the ice-cold pain she felt from them.

And froze in horror when a fleeting vision of the woman with eight eyes appeared once again in her mind. This time the woman smiled; an unearthly smile that stretched from ear to ear, revealing rows of pin-sharp teeth.

So she hadn't been hallucinating, then.

It was time to talk to an expert.

Moments later, she was yelling at Moussa to wake up and get out of bed, pulling back the grubby sheet he used as a sunblock for his bedroom's window and opening its latch for some ventilation. There was much groaning and cursing in response, along with confusion and incredulity that his little sister would dare to wake him up from his much-needed slumber.

Eventually - eventually - a dishevelled Moussa was sitting upright on the side of his bed, with Yatima sat on a crate of beers facing him. As always when in conversion with her brother, her arms were crossed and she had the look of anger and disapproval their mother had always shown him. With no explanation forthcoming for the interruption, he finally raised his open hands in the international gesture for '*What?!*'

"*Tell me* about Anansie," came the blunt reply.

If Moussa could look more confused, he did so then. "Who? Anansie ... what, Anansie the joker? The trickster? What *about* him? Sister, you wake me up for me to-."

"Tell me about him!" Yatima interrupted, sharply. "*La neexee*. It's *important!*"

Not liking the crazy look in his sister's eyes, Moussa did

as instructed. He told her about the stories he used to tell her when she was little, and where the stories had come from (mostly from their mother at bedtime, and from his friends when he was at school). It all tallied up with the things she'd said to Fatou - that Anansie was just a story character for children - nothing sinister.

Yatima pressed on. "But what about the *darker* stories, Moussa - you know anything about them?" She shivered as she asked the next question. "You know anything about an evil-looking ghost lady with eight eyes?"

Moussa laughed. "Sister, Anansie is *male* - he's no lady. And he's not scary; unless your big brother's holding him in front of you, like I used to. I think you got the wrong spider." Noticing that her initial mood had changed from its usual anger to something resembling fear, he reached out to Yatima. "Sister - what's wrong? Tell me everything."

And so Yatima found herself repeating the whole story to her older sibling. She ended by showing him the red marks on her left hand, and wasn't surprised that they had grown and worsened.

Or that she experienced another brief, horrifying vision of the spider lady when she gently probed the wounds one more time.

Moussa was taken aback by the look of sheer terror on his sister's face when the vision happened. Eventually, she composed herself sufficiently to continue talking.

Moussa rolled back on to his bed in thought, before slowly lifting up again to his seated position.

"There is *one* story," he said eventually. "One story from Mangeria, about a spider lady. Old Babou told it to me years ago, over cards one night, but I never heard the spider lady being called Anansie. He said the spider lady was the first - the *mother* - of *all* the spiders ... and that she lives on and on by luring you to her trap, and giving you her gifts when its her time to die. And that day-by-day you become her, a little at a time, until you become the spider lady yourself. And then, after a long, long time living like that, it becomes time for you to pass the gifts on yourself."

A cool breeze blew through the open window at that moment. Looking over, Yatima shuddered to see a silky cobweb that had clung to the windowframe shivering in the wind.

"Well, I'd say it's definitely a spider bite," said Fatou as she concluded her study of Yatima's hand at her medical office. "But it's funny how we never saw it before; I'm sorry I missed it, Yatima. I'm still waiting on the toxicology report from your blood sample, and *you know* how slow things are here. Any fever or nausea?"

"Visions," Yatima replied, flatly. "A woman with eight eyes. Lots of teeth. Terrifying. Starting to get a headache too, I think."

Fatou inhaled deeply. "Well, I'm wary of saying 'hallucinations' to you again. Don't forget I prescribed plenty of rest for you, for getting over that kind of thing. Maybe stay home for the rest of your time off; let your mind sort itself out." She grinned maliciously. "And maybe I can convince Ali to give you another week."

Yatima laughed at this; it felt good to smile. Time to bring up her chat with Moussa. "I've been speaking to my brother, Fatou. You know what he's like with his stories - it's about the only thing he's good at, like I said before. Anyway; he told me about a Mangerian spider lady, and she seems to fit my 'hallucinations'."

Fatou nodded. "Hmm - could be. Maybe you picked up that story without knowing it, burying it deep down until the shock of your bite brought it to the surface. And maybe I shouldn't have mentioned spooky stories in our last conversation. The mind works in funny ways, Yatima, and so do venomous bites."

Fatou looked down at Yatima's hand. "I'm going to give you an anti-venom shot, just in case ... and then you're going to put your feet up and let Moussa run around after you for a change."

Yatima did as Fatou ordered, and spent the next day at home. The hand itched, but the anti-venom jab seemed to help and she did her best not to scratch at the bite marks.

Moussa had planned to get some friends over for another round of late night cards, but a strong word or two from Fatou when she caught him ambling along with a crate of cheap beer outside the hotel compound put him off the idea for a few days longer.

That night, Yatima woke about midnight with a shriek - for clinging to the bedside lamp was a huge, striped spider. Its long, hairy legs wrapped around the curve of the lampshade like a skeletal claw and cast eerie shadows against the bed's headboard, while its bloated body, silhouetted against the illumination of the light bulb, *throbbed* like a freshly torn-out heart. Shuddering uncontrollably while her eyes fixed on the hideous *thing* that had invaded her room, Yatima edged away from the lampshade and leaped down on to the floor.

Something *sticky* tickled at her feet and ankles as she scampered to Moussa's room. She brushed and flicked away the irritating residue with the back of her hand. And shivered when she realised it was *cobwebs*.

Her *brother* could come and deal with the spider, she had decided (dealing with bugs was perhaps the only *other* thing he was useful for) - and, thinking about it, it wasn't impossible that *he* was responsible for it, anyway. With this thought in mind, her fear began to turn to fury.

Finding his room empty, Yatima shouted for him around the house. She soon found him on the front balcony, a beer in one hand and earphones on his head.

"Is this some kind of *joke* to you?" she demanded, still shaking. "Putting *spiders* in my room? You think I'm just a little girl again?!"

Shocked out of his relaxation, Moussa half fell from his chair before claiming all innocence - which didn't sit well with his sister. Stomping back to their kitchen, she grabbed their sweeping brush and thrust it in his hand. "Go and deal with that *thing*!"

Shaking his head in bemusement, he wandered off to her room, before stopping at the open door in shock. "*Yalla*, sister," he called out. "*What* have you been doing?" She followed him and stifled a scream.

The floor of the entire room was coated in thick cobwebs.

In the end, it turned out there was more than one spider in Yatima's room; there were *over a dozen*. How they'd got there was a complete mystery; her window was shut, as had been the door to the rest of the house.

With a groan, Moussa realised his relaxed evening had come to an abrupt ending; his sister would task him with immediately de-bugging her entire room. The job would take him until dawn.

Once the offending creatures had been carefully removed and deposited *well away* from their home, every bedsheet and item of clothing was checked (before being bundled up for laundry), while every corner of the room was investigated and vacuumed. After that, the mattress was beaten and the rickety bedframe was scrubbed with the broom. Then, once Yatima was satisfied her bedroom had been thoroughly cleaned, she set him to task on checking the rest of the house.

Thankfully, no evidence of webbery or spiders could be found elsewhere and, with the onset of sunrise, an overwhelming sense of fatigue overcame Yatima. She chose, however, to sleep on the sofa in the living room (a fact Moussa scowled at after all his cleaning), and by the time the Fajr prayer was being called from the nearest mosque they were both fast asleep.

"Sister, you don't look well."

Lying awkwardly and upside-down on the sofa, Yatima

opened bleary eyes to find a blurry-triplicate of Moussa standing in front of her.

"Euuugh ... I'm *fine*," she mumble-lied. "Just go away, will you?"

"Fatou says I should look after you," he responded, shuddering at the thought of her brief conversation with him the day before.

Yatima groaned. "You want to help? Go stay with your drinking buddy Oumar for a couple of days. Let me rest proper."

"You sure?" Moussa asked in response, but before his sister could respond he was already half-way out the front door with another crate of beer.

I would like to be able to say that a couple of days rest from her brother would be all Yatima needed to aid her recovery. Unfortunately, the previous evening of removing spiders and cobwebs, despite being bizarre and unsettling in its own way, must mark the last evening of 'normality' within Yatima's life, and act as the beginning of something new - for the three days that followed (which were also the last three days of her *human* life) were *anything but* normal.

As if aware of her brother's exit, the eldritch venom in Yatima's bloodstream began to quickly consume and overpower her throughout the morning; in a raging fever, she found she was unable to wake from unsettled slumbers, and moaned and tossed and turned beneath thin sheets she quickly soaked in sweat.

Nightmarish visions of the figure she had begun to call Lady Anansie filled her unending dreams. She clawed and scratched at invisible spiders she imagined to be crawling all over her body, while the bites on her hand throbbed and quivered as if alive; it felt as if something was trying to break through the wounded skin, gnawing away at the meat in its desperate attempt to escape.

The pulsating veins on her left arm were raised high from her flesh and blackened up to and beyond her shoulder, the poison climbing through her blood vessels, up past her throat and across her chest.

Two days after he had left, a drunken Moussa returned. Shuffling into the living room, he choked in horror as his addled brain slowly comprehended the sight in front of him. Yatima was writhing and lifted from the sofa, her back arched and twisted in an unnatural manner. Her skin was a mess of welts and scratches and her eyes - *Yàlla* her eyes - were black, swollen and unblinking, as dark blood leaked from their tear ducts and tiny pinpricks of reflected light glistened off their ebony surface.

And the spiders had returned.

So many of them this time - too many to count. Crawling over Yatima's body, her face, her hair. Thick, sticky webs that had been woven around the sofa so that it was almost unrecognisable beneath the mass of spun silk, countless spiders nonchalantly spinning and weaving as if to create a cradle for his sister.

No. Not a cradle. A cocoon.

Moussa cried out and reached for his sister, intent on grabbing her contorted form away from the hideous nightmare festering in their living room.

It was the last act of his uneventful, beer-sodden life.

Yatima's black, bloated eyes didn't really recognise her

brother. He was merely prey, now. She elegantly twisted her contorted body and pounced on him just as he was lunging toward her to try and aid her.

Rolling her tongue investigatively around her mouth and finding it was now full of the very same razor-sharp pins her Lady Anansie vision possessed, she buried her face deep into the nape of his neck and tore away his throat.

A little too drunk to realise what had happened and far too drunk to resist, Moussa's death was perhaps easier for him than it could have been. She had begun to feed on his blood before he had finished dying.

After an hour of feasting on Moussa, the thing that had once been Yatima found that most of her fever had gone, as had the pain in her left hand and arm.

She felt wonderful, in fact.

Gliding her hand across her brother's face, she gently closed Moussa's eyes. In this way she discovered she was able to spin her *own* web, as a gossamer-thin layer of silk emerged from her fingers and clung to his face, like paint applied by brush to a canvas surface.

Instinct told her to continue in this manner, and soon she had covered Moussa in a paper-thin sheen of silk.

She could return to feeding on him some other day. "Jërejëf, Moussa," she said, finding the rasp of her voice curious. *Thank you.*

For now though, she felt a *beckoning*, to return to the cocoon the spiders had been creating for her; her metamorphosis was not yet complete, she realised. She made to lie down within the bed of webs, but caught a glimpse of herself within the living room's wall mirror - realising there and then that her nightmarish visions had been nothing more than a reflection of what her new self was to become.

"Lady Anansie," she said to herself, her smile stretching from ear to ear.

Time had no meaning for her as she lay beneath the silken veil the spiders had delicately placed over her. *Her* spiders.

Having feasted, the changes that returned to course through her body were *pleasurable* instead of painful. She felt her swollen black eyes separate into four pairs of smaller eyes, while her ribs creaked and distorted to form for her two extra pairs of limbs. Her body extended, and created a toughened exo-skeleton around itself; in time, she'd be able to see the beautiful yellow and black stripes that were forming across her lengthened back.

Her dreams returned, but whereas before they had filled her head and heart with dread they spoke to her now of limitless opportunity; she was *majestic*; the *ultimate* huntress, and smiled at the thought of replacing the infantile stories she had heard as a child with new and terrible stories of her own.

In time she felt the transformation was complete, and easily tore away at the web cocoon surrounding her. Proud of her new physique, she stretched and found her limbs could easily touch the roof and walls within the living room.

It was then that she noticed the old woman from the antique shop, standing in the doorway to the kitchen; bent and huddled beneath her many layers of wraps.

She was carrying the Anansie box in her shrivelled little hands, and gave the thing that had been Yatima - *the new Lady Anansie* - a slow and respectful bow.

"All I have been is within *you* now," the old woman croaked. "I would offer you my flesh, but I am only dust." She placed the Anansie box on the floor at her feet.

"Just one question," the spider woman said. "Why *me?*"

"Because we both wanted *the same thing*," the old woman rasped, as if it were an obvious answer.

"Which is?"

"Why, *more* than you have now, of course," came the reply. "*Always* more. In time you will learn how to lure your prey, and deceive their minds, just as I lured you. You will learn this and a great many other things. And when you have become the dust that I am now, the box will let your spirit pass into another - but that will be many, many years from today. Feast well, Lady Anansie."

And with that, her ancient body gently crumbled and collapsed to the ground.

Lady Anansie crept over to the box, picked it up with one of her new limbs and briefly studied it. She would form a pouch of silk to keep it about her person until she could decide on a safe place for it, she decided.

In the meantime, there was much to do.

Were she to try and mingle unobtrusively amongst her prey, she realised she would need to dress like the old woman, wrapping herself in bundles of layers of shrouding clothing, and living with stealth in the shadows.

She would worry about that later - for now, she would take pride in her new form as she hunted in the night.

If she were vindictive, Ali the concierge would be her next kill. But there was no meat on him. A more practical prey would be Fatou - but she had always been good to her former self, and it would be some time before her semblances of humanity were fully stripped away and she became a *pure* creature without mercy.

No, Xanbaru was a land where people disappeared every day and people seldom noticed - and she had all the time in the world to choose the most succulent prey.

And maybe she would broaden her horizons and travel; Yatima would have *liked* that.

THE END

TIN CAN

The following are a series of communications between cargo vessel ML0204 returning to Luna from Mars and Company Mission Control, over a period of approximately 28 days from 12.04.2081.

DAY 01

Freight vessel ML0204. 04.07am.

Mayday, mayday, this is Co-pilot Jaya Balakrishnan of freight vessel ML0204, travelling inbound from Mars to Luna. Mission Control please respond. We have sustained substantial damage to rear of ship; impacts from what appear to be a micro-meteorite shower. My Pilot Pavol Stanislaw is dead; caught by the impacts. Cargo pods are also believed compromised; I've not yet had chance to evaluate. Life support is holding. Please send Emergency Response Team ASAP. Sending transmission.

DAY 01

Company Mission Control, Luna. 04.43am.

Cargo ship ML0204, this is Mission Control acknowledging your transmission. ERT are primed and ready to launch within an hour; their ETA to you is 31 days. Hang tight, Jaya - they're on their way. In the meantime, please follow protocols; eat and drink well, get your sleep. Good news about the life support. Keep us updated on all the vital stuff. Take your time on the routine tasks and keep talking to us. Sorry to hear about Stanislaw, Jaya. I know it's a gross-out job but you're gonna have to bag him up. If you can give us an update regarding the cargo pod situation that'd be great, but like I said, just take your time on everything; you're our priority now, not the ship. Sending.

DAY O1
Freight vessel ML0204. 06.04am.
Thanks for update, Mission Control; appreciate the quick response. Shame about the time lag as I could really do with some proper conversation right now. I'm going to go deal with Pavel; he wasn't in the gravity tube, so he's floating around back there in the freight area, and it's a mess. I'll have to suit-up because of the impacts. I'll get back to you later about the cargo pods. Sending now.

DAY O2
Freight vessel ML0204. 11.42am.
Jaya here - back again, Mission Control. Okay, Pavel is bagged and tethered; I've got him in the cargo freezer section. Never want to do *that* again. Regarding the pods; it's bad news and good news. Bad news is that they took a bad hit from the shower; I've had to seal them off as they were leaking air. Most of the perishables got hit too, so they'll be unusable. The rest of the cargo was stuff like mineral samples coming home and busted-up mining equipment, so no big problem there. The *good news* is I think I can seal the impact

holes on the ship's outer skin from inside the ship if you need me to; it'd give me something to do. Not essential, but I'll leave it to you to decide. Also, I've just checked food supplies and I'm covered; twice as much food now, unfortunately. This was my first trip out with Pavel, so I didn't know him, but please pass on my condolences to his family.

DAY 02
Company Mission Control, Luna. 01.23pm.
Jaya, thanks for the rundown on everything. Sorry you had to bag-up Pavel; no one should have to do that. We're trying to get hold of his next of kin at the moment; if you need to talk about anything in relation to all that, we're here for you. Regarding the impacts; let's leave those for now, unless you really need a job for distraction. Get yourself some rest; those ships run on auto anyway, so put your feet up and let it drive you home. Oh, last thing - Emergency Response have done the slingshot round Earth so they're on their way. Sending.

DAY 02
Freight vessel ML0204. 02.19pm.
Thanks, Mission Control. Getting some sleep now. Sending.

DAY 05
Company Mission Control, Luna. 00.01am.
Cargo ship ML0204 this is Mission Control. Jaya, is everything okay up there? It's been three days now since last we heard from you and we're getting a little concerned. We're sending this message on repeat until we get a response.

DAY 06

Freight vessel ML0204. 01.13am.

ML0204 here. Sorry. Things have been a little messed up. Not 100% sure what's going on. Will get back to you. Transmission sent.

DAY 06

Company Mission Control, Luna. 02.14am.

Luna here, Jaya. When able to, please can you elaborate on current situation? We may be able to help. Sending now.

DAY 08

Company Mission Control, Luna. 13.50pm.

Company Mission Control here, ML0204. Jaya, it's been another two days since our last brief communique; is it possible you can update on current situation? We've been trying to look in on your videofeeds but they appear to be down. We're here to help if you need us, Jaya. Sending.

DAY 09

Freight vessel ML0204. 15.22pm.

Mission Control, ML0204 here. Request urgent permission to jettison Pilot Stanislaw's body bag. Sending now.

DAY 09

Company Mission Control, Luna. 16.08pm.

Hello Jaya, thanks for the message, we were getting worried there. Please can you give reason for your request to jettison Pilot Stanislaw. Standard protocol is to return deceased to next of kin on Earth, and for autopsy. We hope everything's okay up there, Jaya. Sending.

DAY 09
Freight vessel ML0204. 17.43pm.
There's someone in here with me.

DAY 09
Company Mission Control, Luna. 18.58pm.
Jaya, this is Dr Boehringer from the psych-evaluation team. We received your last transmission, and Jaya, you *know* that can't be the case. You're halfway between Mars and Luna. Please can you advise on your thinking. Sending.

DAY 09
Freight vessel ML0204. 20.03pm.
At first I thought there was an anomaly with the gravity ring, as objects began to move about on their own; food falling off the serving table, that kind of thing. But I've triple-checked everything with the ship's computer and there's no issues. But then I started seeing shadows where there shouldn't be shadows. And shadows *moving*. And I know it sounds crazy but I can feel this 'oppressive presence', and it's only been like this since Pilot Stanislaw died. I can't sleep anymore, as I feel I'm being *watched* all the time. Then for some reason I checked Stanislaw's personal files - I knew he kept his code in his storage locker. I don't know why I did this, it was almost like that presence *wanted* me to do it. Anyway - oh God - his files are full of ... depraved stuff. Videoclips and images of rituals and killings, sacrifices and stuff; he was a sick animal. A beast. I mean really, really sick. And I'm stuck in here with

him. I mean, how the hell did you *employ* someone like that? I'm sending you some files so you can see for yourself. I want that body off the ship. Sending.

DAY 09

Company Mission Control, Luna. 22.13pm.
This is Dr Boehringer again, Jaya, thanks for the update. Files received. Jaya, that's very disturbing about Stanislaw. Security are checking him out now. You're in a situation you really shouldn't be in, and I'm sorry. In regards to everything else you've mentioned, please focus on your training; isolation can cause many kinds of hallucinatory effects and paranoia. We're in debate about the body bag situation, and we'll let you know the decision soon. Please get some rest. Sending.

DAY 10

Freight vessel ML0204. 00.26am.
As you will see from the attached images I'm sending you, the entire ship has been painted with the message 'NO EXIT' hundreds of times over. This has been painted in Stanislaw's blood; I went to sleep for less than an hour and woke up to find this. Help me!!!!

DAY 10

Company Mission Control, Luna. 02.11am.
Jaya, we are evaluating. best thing meanwhile is to keep calm. Keep yourself busy with tasks; immediately set about cleaning off those messages: it's not good for you to see and it's not good for the circuitry. Stay strong, Jaya. Sending.

DAY 10

Company Mission Control, Luna. 07.33am.

Jaya, hi. All clear on the body bag situation. You're free to jettison Stanislaw, if that helps. Hang in there; remember that all your paranoia and experiences have been associated with the body bag, and once it's gone you can feel assured there's no one else there. Dr Boehringer's going to send you some relaxation techniques. One other thing; engineering have said check your air mix; that might explain the hallucinations. Sending.

DAY 11

Freight vessel ML0204. 00.46am.

Not hallucinations! Hallucinations don't *hurt you.* See attached images of bruises sustained over past twenty-four hours. Download videofeed from my suit's cam and you will see me being hurled around the cabin. Please help me!

DAY 11

Company Mission Control, Luna. 12.51pm.

Dr Boehringer here, Jaya. Jaya, we've studied the images and your suit's camerafeed and can only deduce you are self-harming. We *want* to believe you but there's no-one else visible on those images. I want you to take 200mg of Ethylcarbezine from the medipack. Take one three times a day. They'll help you through this, Jaya. When you're feeling calmer we can talk again. Sending.

DAY 12

Company Mission Control, Luna. 00.00am.

Jaya, how are you? Please respond. Over.

Repeats message for 5 days.

DAY 17

Freight vessel ML0204. 03.42am.

Sequence of indistinct images and videofeed sent from ship, but no message.

DAY 17

Emergency Response Team vessel DF902. 11.10am.

Message to Co-pilot Jaya Balakrishnan of freight vessel ML0204, travelling inbound from Mars to Luna. Jaya, this is Commander Zartaloudis of ERT ship DF902 - I've some good news; we've crossed the half-way mark to reach you. We've been updated on your situation from Mission Control and seen the footage you've dispatched. As Dr Boehringer has said, it's all about regaining control, Jaya - I've done isolation training in those tin can ships, so I've got a little knowledge of what you're experiencing; you can contact me whenever you like, and as our proximity increases the time-wait will decrease; it'll feel like we're having a proper conversation, soon enough. If you haven't done so already, try and jettison that body - trust me, you'll feel a whole lot better when you've got that thing off your ship.

DAY 17

Freight vessel ML0204. 12.23pm.

Message from ML0204 to emergency vessel DF902. TURN BACK.

DAY 17

Emergency Response Team vessel DF902. 01.12pm.

Negative to turning back, Jaya. Hang in there. Talk to us.

DAY 17

Freight vessel ML0204. 01.57pm.

ML0204 to emergency vessel DF902. This is NOT Jaya.

DAY 17

Emergency Response Team vessel DF902. 02.54pm.

Jaya, it's our belief you're experiencing severe effects from isolation and the medication you're prescribed may also be affecting you. Remember who you are, Jaya - Co-pilot Jaya Balakrishnan of freight vessel ML0204, travelling inbound from Mars to Luna. I've read your flight record and it's impressive - you can *do* this, Jaya. Talk to us.

Message repeats as no response for two days.

DAY 19

Freight vessel ML0204. 08.13am.

ML0204 to Mission Control and emergency vessel DF902. I have jettisoned Stanislaw's body. It was heavily scarred with what I can only describe as *symbols* when I returned to the freight area; I did NOT make these. They almost look as if they burned out of his skin. I took images with my suitcam and will be sending them with this message. Also, I have looked back on messages sent over the past few days; you're going to think me even crazier than you already do, but I am telling you I did NOT send you those messages. DF902, I look forward to seeing you in 13 days or so. Dr Boehringer, I'll continue on the Ethylcarbezine, but you'll be pleased to hear I feel a weight's been lifted.

DAY 19
Company Mission Control, Luna. 09.41am.
Dr Boehringer here, Jaya. That's excellent news. Glad to hear you're sounding much better. I also have some news for you regarding our ongoing investigation into Pilot Stanislaw - it would appear he was part of some 'occult circle' that had been establishing itself on Mars - we think it is linked to the *Chaos Organisation* that caused so much havoc on Luna about ten years ago. So it seems fortune - and your hard work - have given us a head-start in keeping on top of this situation. That's something to be proud of, Jaya - you're doing an amazing job under the most challenging of circumstances. Keep in touch with us! Sending.

DAY 27
Emergency Response Team vessel DF902. 05.46pm.
Jaya, please come in, it's Commander Zartaloudis. It's been eight days now since we last heard from you. We're only five days from intercepting you. If you can hear me, please hang in there.

DAY 27
Freight vessel ML0204. 06.23pm.
No message was sent, but a disturbing videofeed was received by both the Emergency Response Team and Mission Control. It appeared to show Pilot Stanislaw somehow suspended in mid-air, floating upside-down, in the gravity ring section of

the vessel. His arms were outstretched in the symbol of the cross and he was seen to be shouting in an unidentifiable language. His body appeared to be heavily cut and scarred with runic symbols or hieroglyphs. Co-pilot Balakrishnan was also in the image. She appeared to lying prostrate in front of Pilot Stanislaw, apparently shaking and crying. Ship's inner wall panels appeared to be covered in what has been assumed to be blood.

DAY 27

Emergency Response Team vessel DF902. 06.59pm.
Message to Co-pilot Jaya Balakrishnan. Jaya, this is Commander Zartaloudis. We're ... we're not quite sure what we've just seen on the videofeed that came in. Please can you contact us, if you can. We're thinking of you, Jaya.

DAY 28

Freight vessel ML0204. 02.25am.
Well, I guess that's why the company mainly employs *orphans* for the cargo runs, huh? Less hassle with the families when things go wrong, and it keeps the insurance payouts low. If I wasn't an orphan, I'd be asking you to pass on my goodbyes to my mom and dad right about now. I ... I don't think I'm going to make it, guys. I ... I jettisoned the body, nearly ten days ago. He came back.

DAY 28

Company Mission Control, Luna. 04.32am.
Dr Boehringer here, Jaya. Jaya - we can't imagine what you're going through right now; we can only get a tiny picture of

what's really happening on your vessel. But the Response team are only four days away now; they've already begun their retro-boosting to match speed and align with you. Four days, Jaya, and we'll have you off that ship.

DAY 28
Freight vessel ML0204. 10.40am.
Message was very fragmented and distorted, but has been carefully re-assembled.
Mission Control, this is Jaya. ... My final report. Okay ... I've got maybe an hour of half-decent air left, then I'm sucking my own fumes. ... My very own on-board evil spirit has decided to turn off life support and expel all the oxygen, and I can't override. ... I'm not going out that way because I know what it does to you, so after this call I'm going to blow the emergency escape hatch and maybe walk the rest of the way home without my helmet - it's a quicker way out. ... I've already made the necessary coordinate and trajectory adjustments, so the ship's gonna smack down on Luna's dark side, out of everyone's way. ... Stanislaw's listening, by the way, and he's not happy. ... Commander Zartaloudis, do not - I repeat, DO NOT - intercept the ship and make entry - otherwise I fear you'll be bringing Stanislaw home with you. ... Dr Boehringer; I know your report is going to report everything as a 'metaphysical anomaly' and put me down as having hallucinations on account of the isolation, or oxygen deprivation, or being depressurised, or lack of sleep or - or maybe that I just went plain nuts ... but none of those things throw you round a ship like a rag-doll, or turn off your life support, or terrify you to death. ... Anyway, you've seen all

the images and videofeeds, so you can make up your own mind, if you haven't already, before filing your report. ... At least we now know what a poltergeist does when it's vacuum-sealed in a tin can. Signing off.

THE END

THE SALMON

The spirit of Quentin D'Orsay sat glumly atop the shabby, woodwormed wardrobe in room number twelve of the Golfer's Retreat Hotel; the room in which he'd met his bizarre demise a few hours earlier. It would be fair to say the mood of the deceased was sullen, which is perhaps understandable. With elbows resting on his knees and hands propping up his chin, he watched the team of horrified and bemused Scottish Highland constabulary and forensics officers as they quietly went about their duties and procedures.

Most tried not to look at what remained of his mutilated body, he noticed, as it sat as a squat, deformed *lump* in the centre of the room - though from time to time an officer would inadvertently catch an unwanted glimpse of it before quickly needing to leave for a lungful of fresh air.

The manner of D'Orsay's murder had been 'beyond horrific' (a matter we shall come to later) though he was, for now at least, free from the agony and suffering he had endured at the hands of his murderer. I say 'for now' because although he was now most definitely *dead*, Mr D'Orsay's killer had unfortunately promised to return and 'collect' his soul the following evening - and based on all that had transpired thus far with his assailant, Quentin D'Orsay had no reason to believe this wouldn't happen.

Escape was impossible, he had quickly deduced; his phantom self appeared to be bound to the confines of the four walls of the hotel room, and (though he had certainly tried on numerous occasions over the past few hours) he had been unable to pass through the open door to the hotel hallway outside.

Nothing for Quentin D'Orsay to do then, but wait for his fate to arrive, watch as the police continued their solemn business, and mull over the events that had led to this grisly affair ...

There had been D'Orsays attending Oxford for generations, and like many of his illustrious predecessors Quentin D'Orsay had majored in Literature Studies. Unlike Quentin however, those same predecessors had all 'made a good name' for themselves - as successful writers and novelists in their chosen fields, and had in turn received the respect of their peers and the general public alike. Each and every one had been successful on account of three things; *diligence*, *hard work* and *natural talent*.

Lacking all three of these, Quentin had resorted to living off the family name in order to 'pull strings' and bag reasonably-well-paid jobs as a journalist on Fleet Street.

For years he'd swanned from one tabloid job to the next, spending much of his time 'researching a good story' down the ale houses frequented by others in his trade - 'journos' (journalists), 'smudgers' (photographers) and the variety of unsavoury types from all walks of life who - for the right amount of money - would give him salacious tip-offs on the latest gossip; gossip he could quickly pass off as *legitimate news articles* for his newspaper.

Now, Quentin was the kind of person who used be referred to as a cad, or a scoundrel, or a 'bad sort'. He looked somewhat *debonair*, which helped him enormously; tall, suited, aristocratic and with a pearly smile he somehow managed to keep a brilliant white (despite the tobacco he constantly smoked and alcohol he regularly swigged). When he wasn't 'researching' down the pubs, he'd put his charm to use elsewhere; a quick fling with an editor's wife, perhaps, or a (usually disastrous) liaison with one of the typists at the newspaper.

If Quentin wasn't so self-centred he would see that his life wasn't a bad one (for him at least) - and *so what* if his scandalous little newspaper stories damaged reputations or ruined a few innocent lives?

Eventually, the editor of whichever publication he was working for at the time would see through this undeniable charmer and catch on to his foppish, work-shy routine. Then he'd be packed off to a *rival* newspaper, to give *them* a year or two of grief instead.

This indolent, carefree way of life would have carried on unchanged until all the newspapers of Fleet Street had grown tired of his ill behaviour - were it not for a seemingly chance encounter with a somewhat nervous, bespectacled individual down one of Quentin's favourite ale houses one cold, wet and rainy Friday evening.

I say 'a seemingly chance encounter' because the individual in question was *exactly* the kind of person Quentin was on the look out for at that moment in time - there was no 'chance' about it. For if D'Orsay had any talent at all, it was for following his nose when it came to finding someone who could *do most of his work for him*, which would make his own life even easier than it already was.

Indeed, that was the sole reason Mr D'Orsay had managed to remain so long within Fleet Street. For example, when he'd worked at the *Daily Albion* he'd charmed the girls in the typing pool into writing up all his articles (usually at the eleventh hour, before the paper was due to go to press). Then during his brief stint at the *Morning Record* he'd bribed a sub-editor into writing up all his pieces (Quentin had discovered the sub-editor was having an affair and Quentin, as you may have worked out for yourself by now, was the sort of rascal to exploit such nuggets of lascivious information).

So within five minutes of conversation with this awkward little fellow (who had been sitting with a hefty pile of books in the corner of the public house) D'Orsay realised he had - once again - found another highly exploitable person; a person named Alexander Figgis.

"What are you writing there, old chap?" quizzed Quentin by way of introduction, as he slid on to the nearest seat without invitation and began peering at the jotting pad in front of the other man.

"O-Oh, nothing much, really," Mr Figgis nervously responded in his mild Scots accent, as he put down his pen. "Bits and bobs, observations about things I find interesting. I-I just like to write, that's all. I've been attending job interviews all week, and was at the *Record* for one this afternoon - but nothing doing there, I don't think."

Of course the Record wouldn't take you on, thought D'Orsay spitefully, *not a timid little shrew like you.*

Quentin studied the other man, like a hawk studies its prey before a kill; he was smaller, as mentioned, and dressed in a threadbare tweed suit. Rounded spectacles; *probably a socialist.* Hmm. Slightly malnourished complexion and gherkin lips. Supping on a half pint of cheap bitter. *Down on his heels; easy to abuse.* Probably staying in some flea-bitten bedsit. Red hair like copper wire on the top of his head, and lots of it. D'Orsay *despised* red hair; it spoke of mad Celts and Rob Roy and pointless insurrection. Something he'd have to tolerate, he sighed to himself inwardly, if he was going to make best use of this scribbler.

"Ah, so ye're a *Scoats*man, eh?" D'Orsay chuckled, with a crass Englishman's interpretation of his dialect. "A wee bit south o' *Glasgae*, are we no'?"

Figgis tried to stammer he was actually from a little island *far, far north* of Glasgow, but D'Orsay overrode him without interest.

"Mind if I take a look?" the taller man continued, as he casually took Figgis's notepad from the top of his pile of books and browsed through its contents. The writing was *superlative*; he picked up on that after reading just a few paragraphs. Of course, he'd never tell this grubby little fellow as much.

I suppose you could say at this point that Figgis seemed somewhat *transfixed* by D'Orsay; his charming smile, the confident manner, the Saville Row suit. Figgis offered a hand. "A-Are you a writer yourself, Mister-?"

"D'Orsay," the Englishman replied, deliberately ignoring

the hand. "*Quentin* D'Orsay." He chuckled a little once more. "And I *D'Orsay* you've heard of me, if you've just come from the *Morning Record*?"

Apparently ashamed that he hadn't, Figgis said nothing, and sheepishly looked down at the remains of his half pint of bitter.

"No?" continued D'Orsay, as he turned the pages of the jotter. "Well, never mind. I was one of - ahem - *the* main features columnist during my stint there. But not really my type of rag, the *Record*, so I thought I'd move on. You know how it is."

Figgis looked impressed. "Who are you working for now, Mr D'Orsay?"

"The *Excelsior*," Quentin replied, jutting out his chin and noting the awe and admiration in the other man's eyes. "Oh, yes - *there's* a quality paper, and no mistake."

D'Orsay went on in this manner for a while, boasting about the celebrities and politicians he interviewed on a regular basis, the exclusives and scoops he'd covered. He neglected to mention that all his articles were mere 'filler' pieces, consigned to the mid-section of the publication, and he'd never made it any closer to the front page than page seven. He noticed the other man go silent, taking in all the waffle he was feeding him. Soon it'd be time to strike the killing blow and sign him up, but not just yet.

Something bright and shining caught D'Orsay's eye, poking out between some of Figgis's books. He tried to ignore it as he continued to brag, but in the end found he had to break off and investigate. Try as he might, he *really couldn't ignore* the object as it glinted; flickering flames from the nearby fireplace causing it to have an unnatural *shimmering* quality. It was half-way down the assortment of notepads and textbooks stacked on the table in front of Figgis, and was attached to what looked like a worn leather book.

"*What's this*, old chap?" asked D'Orsay as he made a lunging beeline for it. "Looks a little unusual."

"Ah, now I'd rather you didn't," Figgis responded, with a firmness to his voice he'd lacked thus far. "That's something of a *personal* project." Figgis made to grasp at the leather article, but D'Orsay's lunge caused the pile of books to collapse, scatter and fall about their feet.

In this way D'Orsay saw that what he'd taken to be a leather book could better be described as a *folio* or file containing single leaf pages. Each page was held in place by the shining silver clasp which, on closer inspection, was shaped like a stylised fish. The impact of the fall had caused the clasp to spring open, and some of the pages had slipped from the folio. Ignoring the other fallen books, Figgis immediately went for these single sheets, but again D'Orsay beat him to it.

"May as well take a look, now it's open," he said victoriously. Figgis eyed him with a glacial stare in response.

Each leaf was thick and grainy, Quentin observed - almost like parchment or papyrus. At the head of the sheets were beautifully detailed ink illustrations of people; almost like Victorian cameos but with a sketched intensity that was lacking in the austere linearts of the nineteenth century. If this Alexander Figgis had drawn these then he had as much talent as an illustrator as he had as a writer.

There were images of both young persons and old, male

and female - and beneath the drawings were paragraphs of text written in sublime calligraphic script. Tiny notes and additions were applied in the columns of space beside the main text, along with intricately drawn symbols. Some of these Quentin recognised as renditions of naturalistic, elemental figures; trees, the sun and moon, a hare, a fox and so forth, and some seemed more astrological in style. Even a bullish rogue like D'Orsay was impressed at the skill and craftsmanship that had gone into each page, and grudgingly he told Figgis as much. But one thing troubled him, however; "I can't read a word of it, old boy. What is it; some kind of Gaelic gibberish?"

Figgis noticeably cooled at this. "If you like," he replied eventually. "It's a tongue spoken only on the island I'm from. These pages are a family tree, in a way; a record of certain ... ancestral individuals of the island."

D'Orsay flicked to the last page, and his eyes rested on an ominous-looking figure. He had raven-dark hair hanging about his shoulders and grim facial features that seemed to leap from the page in their severity. "Now *he's* someone you wouldn't want to meet on a dark and stormy night," Quentin quipped.

"No," replied Figgis quietly, as he quickly snapped the clasp shut on the folio and began bundling up his books and notes, "you wouldn't."

It looked as if the little Scotsman had had enough and was making to leave, so D'Orsay quickly steered the conversation back the way he wanted it to go. "You know," he said, with all his oily charisma, "I've always need of a good man to back me up on the features column at the *Excelsior*."

Figgis looked up warily from his book gathering. "And what - you're ... thinking of me?"

"Well, why not?" D'Orsay replied breezily, slapping him on the shoulder. "I can see that you can write a bit, and you look like the sort who would never let me down. It's ... *tough* work at times, with all sorts of barmy hours - but think of the *prestige*, man! Getting to write for the *Excelsior*!"

There was a very lengthy pause, and then a smile erupted on Figgis's face that made Quentin shrivel; *that man needs dental work*, he shuddered to himself. But the nervous little man seemed genuinely impressed with the idea, despite being able to mumble little more than "I can't believe it. Articles by Alexander Figgis in the *Excelsior*!"

D'Orsay shifted awkwardly at the suggestion of this grubby fellow actually getting his own name in the rag. "Well, *in time* you'll get your name in there, old chap ... but for now, let's just keep things ... *off* the official ledger, eh? Those bods in charge at the paper won't just take *anyone* on, even with the official sanction of myself. No, ah ... best for now I take you under my wing *unofficially*, so to speak - teach you the ropes, and all that."

"Oh, whatever you say, Mr D'Orsay," Figgis replied, his apparently stunned demeanour now replaced with another beaming grin, "whatever you say!"

His victim assured, D'Orsay smiled like a snake that'd just downed a fattened rat. "Very well then," he continued. "Now ... I suppose I'd better elaborate a little on the suggested partnership." Figgis was all ears now, unblinking in his attentiveness. D'Orsay had him on the hook, all right.

"Thing is, old chap, as I'm sure you can understand, a

high profile columnist like myself doesn't always have time to do all that needs to be done in my line of work. My infernal editor expects me to sniff out a story, chase it up, work on getting an exclusive interview with the main protagonists, make all the arrangements to keep my interviewee ticketyboo and cosy so they'll spill the beans ... and after all that I've to rush back home and write it all up in time for the next issue's print deadline; it's a *monstrous* amount of work, dear boy - utterly monstrous." D'Orsay chuckled inwardly again; this little kilt-wearer was lapping it all up. "Anyway, that's where *you'd* come in, dear fellow."

Quentin moved closer, his voice lowering to a conspiratorial whisper. "I'll handle all the tedious stuff - the interviews and so on - and you can be my *unseen partner*, so to speak - taking a quick phone call from me when I've got the story in the bag, then typing it up in time for the next day's print run. What do you say, old bean?"

As I'm sure you've gathered by now, Figgis took the bait and said yes.

And soon Quentin had worked out a system that suited him very nicely indeed. From that day on he never once had to put pen to paper - and soon got his name - *and his name alone* - in bold type as the writer of the best front page articles for the *Excelsior* - along with fame, fortune and a great deal more - all thanks to Alexander Figgis's excellent writing.

But let's not jump ahead of ourselves.

After concluding this most unsavoury of deals with Mr Figgis, Quentin immediately slipped off into the night for a quick drinkie at a gentleman's club he frequented (he certainly had no intention of drinking with that little ginger, now that he'd made him one of his menial staff members).

He toasted himself with a whisky or two, sloped around the club for a while (earwigging on the conversations of the Members of Parliament and other influential types who frequented the club) then made his way back to his Islington apartment.

His happy dreams that night were full of thoughts of offloading his workload on to naive, innocent underlings - all of them desperate for any morsel of work he would dangle above them, in the hope it would get them one step further up the career ladder. He felt like a fisherman, dangling worms just above the water so the fish couldn't reach them.

His subconscious thoughts turned eventually to Figgis; little red-faced, copper-haired Figgis, with his worn out tweedy suit, his social awkwardness, his pathetic little half-pint of bitter and those notebooks scattering everywhere, sending that mysterious leather folio skittering on to the floor.

Ah, *the folio*. The ebb and flow of his dreams began to rest on the folio. He pictured himself carefully undoing the fish-shaped clasp once more, and delicately opening the leathery binder to reveal the contoured, parchment-like sheets within. He slowly rubbed the sheets between his fingers, savouring them; there was something about their texture he couldn't quite place. Every sheet was just as he remembered them; those beautiful ink illustrations at the top of each page, with that stunningly ornate writing underneath.

He continued to turn each page in his dream, soaking up as much information as he could grasp; images of a wan, juvenile girl, a stocky woman of middle-age, a wizened old man. Page after page after page. The words beneath meant nothing still; every paragraph written in that Gaelic nonsense.

He turned the penultimate page and reached the final sheet; the silhouette of that brooding man again, dark and ominous. Penetrating eyes, and waves of long, dark hair that cascaded beyond the stern man's shoulders. Hardened features and the look of malice and contempt that seemed to call out mockingly to him. The wiry arms and hands - he hadn't noticed the hands before - all sinewy and claw-like.

In the pallid, moonlight colours of his dream they seemed to move, those hands; long, powerful fingers and nails, stretching out wide as if rising from a rippling page. The dreaming D'Orsay choked suddenly, feeling those powerful hands about his throat, grasping at him, clawing and pawing at him; one hand pushing his head backwards and the other climbing spider-like upwards and forcing thick fingers into his mouth, to drag at his lower jaw and stretch his jaws apart.

Through the pain, Quentin heard the man speak; six dreaded words in a gravel tone that he would hear again and again for the rest of his life. "I'll be hunting ye, Little Fish."

Other faces appeared suddenly; black, unblinking eyes in silent masks of fish, hare, fox, deer and other wild beasts - all studying him with blank curiosity as more hands came to claw at him and tether him down. As the long-haired man pulled at his face they grabbed at his hair, the fish-masked figure suddenly jabbing at his bare forehead with a red-hot branding rod, marking him with a fish symbol that was identical in style to the clasp on Figgis's folio.

D'Orsay yelped and screamed and fought back, and the figures retreated, laughing - but he was unable to break the powerful hands of the long-haired man. He kept on forcing

Quentin's jaws yet further apart until, with a sickening crack, they broke apart and Quentin's lower jaw became a mush of useless, dangling bone and pulped flesh.

His screams became muffled as his breaths struggled through constricted airways, yet *still* his jaws were being torn wider apart and then - oh God - *something hideously cold* and *flapping* and *slithering* was being forced down into the gaping chasm what was once his face and mouth. The strong, immovable fingers pushed down one after the next of these writhing, squirming things, making Quentin choke and gag and retch, but there was no let up - just more and more of those cold, hideous shapes being rammed into what was left of his throat. And soon he could feel them twisting and slithering *inside* him, and *still* the grim-faced man forced down yet more and more in an unrelenting nightmare.

A nightmare. That's all it was.

Gasping and screaming aloud, Quentin rose up from his bed, soaking in sweat and shaking in terror.

But it would not be the last time he would have that dream.

In order to get the best exclusives, Quentin quickly cultivated an enormous social network across high society London; he'd already done much of the groundwork in the past when the other gullible fools he'd had working for him had been slaving away, and now he had Figgis on board, it would be fair to say that Quentin's success went *meteoric*.

His life became one endless parade of discreet liaisons with politician's wives, daughters of millionaire industrialists and gangster's molls, secret affairs with the mistresses of minor royals and female dignitaries from overseas - and at the end of each day of debauchery, carousing, drinking, eating and living a life of hedonism beyond all imaginings, he'd make a quick call to Figgis with a few words of salacious gossip he'd picked up during his revelry, and leave the rest to him.

And at first, Figgis didn't appear to mind at all; he seemed thrilled at being part of the game and told Quentin he marvelled at how he managed to come up with so many tidbits of scandal night after night.

He timidly mentioned that it rankled him a little when he popped down to the paper stall to see Quentin's name on the articles and not his own, but in response Quentin always quickly reminded Figgis he would never have got the opportunity to write for the *Excelsior* were it not for himself. No, advised D'Orsay, it was best if Figgis 'sucked up' any selfish feelings of resentment and displeasure, for the sake of their partnership.

Once things were rolling along nicely, Quentin set Figgis up in a grubby little flat, some twelve floors up in a residential tower block, and then pretty much *left him there.*

Their system worked as follows; D'Orsay would phone around eleven pm (or often much later), and drunkenly slur to Figgis whatever snippet of gossip he had acquired that evening. Figgis would then be expected to feverishly type up the inebriated monologue into the kind of scandalous story that made newspapers whizz off the shelves. Then, once completed, Figgis would phone the completed story through to the *Excelsior* in order for the article to make the morning edition. And that was it.

Both D'Orsay and Figgis would be sound asleep by the time the morning edition came out (and while the repercussions of their scandalous stories shook the nation's readers). And then, just as their readers were settling down for a night in front of the television, they'd get up and do it all over again.

There *was* a shadow on Quentin's horizon, however; a shadow that took the form of everything associated with *Figgis's folio*. In brief, he just couldn't stop *thinking* about it.

He'd find himself absent-mindedly doodling its fish-shaped clasp on napkins whilst he waited for dessert in restaurants, or spend hours alone trying to recap all of the hand-drawn individuals he'd glanced at whilst leafing through its contents.

And then, of course, there were the nightmares; he'd have a terrifying reprise of the dream about the long-haired, grim-faced man and the animal mask faces at least once a week, and with each repetition its details would become more and more refined and realistic instead of less so.

Worst of all were those six little words the man had said in the dream; "I'll be hunting ye, Little Fish." For some reason these had burned themselves deep into Quentin's consciousness, and he would yelp in fear at the most inconvenient of moments throughout the day or night when they decided to surface in his thoughts.

Occasionally, he'd surreptitiously ask Figgis about the folio; that was, after all, the origin of his neuroses. In return he would receive equally surreptitious responses; on one occasion Figgis said he kept it in a bank deposit box for safe keeping, whereas the next time he was asked he said he'd returned it to his family residence in Scotland. Third time he was asked Figgis tried to make light of it, pretending to have all-but forgotten about the folio. Quentin thought the truth was closer to home, however; he suspected Figgis always kept it nearby, just like when he'd seen him coveting it in the public house, and guessed he probably had something of a dependency on it that was similar to his own.

And slowly but surely, the issue of the folio began to create a bit of a wedge between the two of them.

That matter aside, all was, as I mentioned, going swimmingly for Quentin. He became rather famous, and rather rich; a celebrity in his own right. To add to his nocturnal work schedule he started popping up on television chat shows and radio programmes, and received an endless number of invites to celebrity galas and the like.

He soaked up all the credit and accolades thrown his way, loving every minute of it - and began to *resent* the agreed eleven pm routine of having to phone 'that grubby little Trotskyite Scotsman' in order to maintain his new, more affluent and influential status quo.

Inevitably, things had to turn sour. As D'Orsay's scandalous stories grew, so too did the *Excelsior's* number of readers - which meant the *Excelsior's* editor demanded more of the same. Much more. The paper hired more reporters, but nobody had the social connections Quentin had and nothing matched the sublime quality of Figgis's scandalous stories.

Between them they toppled politicians, revealed the love interests of several royals (British and otherwise), told the world about the secret children of some of Hollywood's top stars and almost caused a Middle Eastern war with their revelations about a Saudi Prince. D'Orsay's once nightly phone calls became almost hourly updates due to the editor's pressure on them, and Figgis found himself churning out article after article for the newspaper; barely able to leave the impoverished flat Quentin had set him up in, and never being paid enough by his increasingly degenerate 'business partner'.

As well as becoming an alcoholic wreck, D'Orsay soon ran up considerable debts at a couple of Mayfair casinos, not to mention several five star hotels in Kensington and Belgravia, and had to pay 'hush-money' to an increasing number of his disgruntled 'love-interests'.

One afternoon there was a rap at the door of Quentin's apartment. It was a telegram from his editor, advising him of several facts. Fact one; his phone didn't seem to be working (a hungover D'Orsay had slept through its endless ringing). Fact two; someone called 'Figgis', who had claimed to be working for both Mr D'Orsay and the newspaper, had suffered a nervous breakdown from apparent overwork, and was at the local infirmary. Fact three; Quentin's final article (a scandalous piece on freemasonry) had somehow missed its deadline. Fact four; Quentin was to come to the editor's office immediately.

Quentin's world had suddenly collapsed.

Rather than go in for questioning and admit to the

unpleasant 'partnership' he'd tricked the naive Mr Figgis into agreeing to, Quentin's response was to go straight to the hospital ward and furiously assault the unfortunate Scotsman for having failed him.

There, of course, was *the folio*, which had now grown considerably fatter in content since D'Orsay had last seen it - Figgis had obviously been spending his spare time working on it. In desperation, Quentin tried to make a grab for it, and a scuffle ensued - Quentin just *had* to have it - and would most likely have won it were it not for the intervention of the ward's enormous matron and a couple of doctors.

Reluctantly, Quentin left; to plan his next move and to work out how to survive the inevitable meeting with his editor. A call was made to the newspaper's office, and a meeting set for late the following day.

By the time Quentin was sat in front of his editor's desk, however, Figgis had packed his meagre belongings and taken the long train journey back to the village from whence he came.

"So you see, I'm afraid I'm as much in the dark about this 'Figgis' character as you are," lied Quentin, as he languidly sat back in his chair and took a long drag from his cigarette. "I'd completed that freemasonry article as scheduled, and had dispatched it to you via courier - though it sounds, regretfully, as if it got lost in transit. My suspicion about 'Figgis' is he's some kind of confidence trickster, trying to sneak himself on to the office's payroll. If you were you, Albert, I'd get the police down to the infirmary and get him checked out."

Albert Bourne, Quentin's editor, was a hulking slab of a man, who gave away very little when it came to anything in life. On this occasion, however, he was in a position to be rather generous with Mr D'Orsay, and slid a piece of paper across his desk for Quentin to read.

It was another telegram, this time from Figgis. It read as follows;

Mr D'Orsay.
I am returning home.
All transcripts of work undertaken given to Mr Bourne.
Flat key also enclosed.
ps. I have the folio.

As Quentin finished reading, Mr Bourne revealed a number of plain brown envelopes, each one stuffed with pages of Figgis's handwritten and typed news articles. Once he was assured that Quentin had visually digested what was in front of him, Mr Bourne also placed the key to Figgis's flat on to the desk.

"I think your little games *up*, D'Orsay," Mr Bourne said, with a quiet sigh. "Now, the way I see it, I have two options. Option one is I immediately fire you, sue you, and turn you into the leading story on tomorrow's front page; the shame on your family's name and reputation will be catastrophic, I suppose. Most likely you'll also end up serving a jail sentence. Option two - and you're probably not going to like this one, knowing what an *arrogant little weasel* you are - is that you get your deceitful backside on a train up north, and go and fetch that little Scottish fellah back here. It sickens me to say this, but your odious little partnership with that man has transformed the fortunes of this newspaper, and I'll be damned if I'm going to let that slip away. You will tell him he'll be well paid by the paper, and well looked after. And that *you'll* be kept on a leash in future. If *you* don't want to do it, I'll get the paper to contact him and make him an offer; I'm sure he'd work well with one of the other journos; Winstanley or Cripps, for example. So make your choice."

Throughout all this, Quentin had gone sheet white.

"But I don't even know where he *lives*!" was the best he could blurt out.

"Oh, I can help you there," smiled Mr Bourne. "After we received that telegram, we called the infirmary for some background information on Figgis. He was a bit of an enigma; no records on file, that kind of thing. However, he did tell one of the nurses that he was going straight back to some island called *Creag Dhubh*, way up north. The hospital weren't happy about him discharging himself so quickly - especially after what they described as a work-induced attack of the nerves - but they said he looked remarkably better in himself, once he'd arranged for that telegram to be sent to us. It's very handy, you know, working in a newspaper; *amazing* what you can find out."

Four hours later, Quentin was on the overnight sleeper train to Glasgow.

It would have been best to avoid Quentin's vicinity in the hours that followed; a cornered rabid dog couldn't have been more vicious.

Drinking heavily, D'Orsay mulled everything over as the train slowly snaked its way northwards. Oh, he'd go and get Figgis alright, and *scalp him* for the humiliation he'd made Quentin endure. Then he'd drag that ginger little worm by the ear all the way back to London, and make sure there were no more of these dubious 'nervous breakdowns' - D'Orsay *knew* people who could *exert pressure* on Figgis to make sure he churned out the goods, and who'd ensure there was no more slipping back to Bonnie Scotland when the going got tough.

Satisfied with his scheme, Quentin proceeded with his immediate plan of drinking all night, and *thanked God* the night train meant he didn't have to look at mile after mile of grim northern factories and belching chimneys.

Unfortunately, he hadn't counted on passing out at 10pm, or the nightmare that followed ...

Once more the dream returned; unlocking the shining, fish-shaped clasp of the folio, caressing the parchment sheets and soaking up all the beautifully mysterious drawings and calligraphic writing. Turning to the final page and feeling the intense glare of the grim-faced man, like being seared by desert sun. Watching helplessly as those powerful hands began to rise from the page and crawl up his neck and face, pulling at his jaw and forcing it to break. The soulless eyes of the grasping, laughing, masked figures and the burning of the firebrand on his naked forehead. The gagged screaming as those writhing, slithering things were relentlessly jammed into what remained of his mouth. The deep, gravelled words of the grim man ringing in his ears; "I'll soon *have* ye, Little Fish."

His repeated screams as he woke brought consternation and alarm from the adjoining sleeping cabins; two pyjamaed passengers and a guard needed to break open the door to see what all the commotion was about.

Once D'Orsay had finally calmed and had assured everyone he was well-enough to be left on his own, he sat shivering in his bed, unable to sleep any further until dawn began to creep around the edges of the window blind. But of greatest consternation to him was the line of wet footprints that led from his bed to the door.

Once he'd arrived in Glasgow, Quentin needed to make two rail connections before arriving at Droichead Cloiche station, the closest railway stop and town to the island of Creag Dhubh.

He arrived at Droichead Cloiche by the end of the afternoon; somewhat dishevelled and, it has to be said, somewhat less wracked with thoughts of revenge - for the time being at least. For now, he just wanted to eat and get a good night's sleep; he could start dealing with Figgis in the morning.

The only accommodation in the area was the Golfer's Retreat Hotel, close to the sea, and he arranged for a taxi to take him there. He was settled into room number twelve; a slightly draughty en-suite with antique fittings and furnishings, but with a rather stunning panoramic view of the ocean - and of Creag Dhubh island.

Before she left, Quentin questioned the thick-set hotelier who had shown him to his room. She confirmed the island was indeed Creag Dhubh (and tried to correct him in his pronunciation of it), and confirmed when asked that a ferry service ran to and fro between the island, from a ferry dock half a mile away. He also asked if she knew anyone from the island with the surname Figgis, which caused a blank. Ferguson, perhaps, or Fitzroy and Fraser, but no Figgis. "But they've a strange twist on the Gaelic tongue, on Creag Dhubh," she furthered, "so perhaps *Figgis* was an island version of another name." Not thinking to tip her for her assistance, D'Orsay asked her to book dinner for him downstairs at seven, and for a copy of the *Excelsior* the next morning with breakfast - then shooed her out of the room.

The rest of the evening was fairly uneventful for Quentin. He briefly studied Creag Dhubh through the window with a glass or two of whisky, and deduced he'd find Figgis within a day - the island looked *tiny*. He then dumped what few essentials he'd fetched into the woodwormed wardrobe and called the *Excelsior*, to leave a message that he'd arrived at his destination and that he was confident of heading back in a day or two. Or maybe three or four. *No rush*, he decided, as he admired the smokey flavours of the third Scotch he'd just poured himself.

Dinner was equally unremarkable, in Quentin's opinion. A half-decent steak, with stodgy pudding dessert. While he was down in the bar later that evening, he asked around to see if anyone knew of Figgis, but again drew a blank.

He was given some handy details about the island, however. It had three small villages, and only one was accessible by automobile - you could only reach the other two by *tractor*, or on foot.

The second village stood beside a strong river that ran down from the hills at the north of the island, had the only public house on the island, and was reputedly very good for salmon fishing.

The third was little more than a few croft cottages to the west, housed by a handful of hardy sheep-rearers, and was reputedly very hard to reach for much of the year. Oh, and (perhaps most importantly) the ferry left at 10.30am each day.

The next morning, Quentin was relieved to find he'd slept well the night before, but was quietly *furious* to discover the *Excelsior* had run his own freemasonry story - *with Winstanley's name on it*! However, he told himself he was going to remain the epitome of calm until the day's task was complete - he was going to down a decent breakfast and a couple of coffees, catch the ferry, find Figgis and charm him into coming back to London. And grab that damned *folio*. And then, once that little runt was back in London where D'Orsay wanted him, the real fun would begin ...

I'm going to skim through the rest of what happened during the day, as the night is perhaps more interesting. Quentin did indeed have his decent breakfast and coffees, and made it on time to the ferry - only to find it would be delayed due to adverse weather. This meant shuffling back to the hotel and waiting for fours hours until the 'swell' had calmed. This delay risked the possibility of having to stay overnight on the island, but he was sure that the public house the locals had mentioned in village number two could put him up if really necessary.

I could tell you the jawdropping beauty of this corner of the world instantly left its mark on D'Orsay as he journeyed across the stretch of water to Creag Dhubh, but you know by now that would be untrue. Finding a quiet spot under cover, he huddled up with a bottle of Scotch he'd pilfered from the hotel bar, and waited to make landfall.

Once there, he strutted off to the first village (there were no taxis available, nor were any necessary as it was close to the harbour) and started asking around about Figgis. Again, this drew blanks, until he chanced upon the island's one police constable, late in the afternoon - who recognised the unflattering description Quentin gave him of Figgis's appearance.

It sounded remarkably like the proprietor of the public house in Taobh Na H-Aibhnethe, the second village, advised the constable, though D'Orsay would have to either walk there or grab a lift on a tractor.

A minute or so later, Quentin was marching off in the direction he'd been given.

And so it was that, early in the evening and with a full moon just rising over the horizon Mr D'Orsay came upon Mr Figgis, as he thrust open the doors of the Geàrr Agus Gealach public house and made his way inside. Figgis was standing behind the bar, casually serving drinks to his patrons as folk music, singing and raucous laughter rang around the packed room.

Their eyes met.

Up to this point, Quentin had expected shock and a fair degree of panic from Figgis, were his search to prove successful. However, it was *he* who would be in for the surprise.

"Mr D'Orsay!" Figgis called out cheerily over the hubbub. "You've made it at last!" Heads briefly turned and a cheer went up, before the villagers went about their merrymaking.

Wary and confused, Quentin slowly waded his way through the locals to the bar, where Figgis poured him a large whisky.

"I-I didn't expect you to -" began Quentin, but Figgis shook his head dismissively.

"Too *loud* in here," Figgis laughed. He indicated toward a quiet alcove of the room, passed the serving duties over to one of the locals and merrily led Quentin away.

D'Orsay immediately noticed a change had come over Figgis, as he cautiously sat down with him. Gone was the nervous, threadbare, stammering little scribbler he'd met in that ale house on Fleet Street. This new Figgis seemed much more confident; *taller* even. Thanking him for the drink, Quentin thought it best to get straight down to business.

"Listen, old chap, I'm awfully sorry the way things turned out back in the Big Smoke, and so's the newspaper. We all feel jolly wretched about it. I'm afraid I went through a bit of a rough patch back there; trouble sleeping, and all that. Went a bit off the rails too, so to speak. Funnily enough, I think it was something to do with that mysterious *folio*. Anyway, the thing is, the newspaper's dreadfully keen on you, old boy, and they thought it best if they sent me in person to tell you they'll do all they can to bring you back in the fold, so to speak. Worth your while *financially*, believe you me!"

D'Orsay went on in this manner for quite some time, fawning at times and dangling fat, financial carrots at others. Figgis watched him intently, never saying a word and letting him prattle on until he finally ran out of steam and things to say. After a final "So what do you say, old bean?" from Quentin, Figgis finally spoke.

"Sounds tempting. And I'll take Mr Bourne up on his offer, *eventually*; this community needs every penny it can get and a few years of me working for the *Excelsior* on London money will pay for a great many things these people could never afford themselves." He looked around at the partying throng. "These are my clan, Mr D'Orsey; my family. Generation after generation. And I'll do anything it takes to make sure they're taken care of."

Figgis really *did* look different, thought Quentin, but put it to the back of his mind in order to focus on showing some faux relief and gratitude. "Well, that's cracking news, old boy," he replied joyfully, "absolutely cracking! We'll get the *Excelsior* kissing our feet again in no time! But you said *eventually* - is there a prob-?"

"Oh, there's no problem," interjected Figgis, "but there's just a wee bit of business to attend to first. I think it's about time you had a proper look at *the folio*, don't you?"

At this, D'Orsay's heart skipped a beat.

While Figgis was away fetching the mysterious folio, D'Orsay took a look around the ale house (*and was Figgis his real name? He doubted it - Quentin made a mental note to ask when he felt on safe grounds with the man*).

The pub was your bog-standard rural drinking establishment, in Quentin's eyes; dusty wooden beams, lots of faded old photos, trophies and horseshoes plastered all over the walls and an enormous glowing hearth that was big enough to roast an elephant on. Not to mention the local toothless simpletons and their relentless 'diddly-diddly' fiddle music. Yes, *very* bog-standard.

There was also an abundance of fishing-related ephemera; rods, stuffed prize catches and the like (he vaguely recalled the adjacent river rattling its way down the hill when he headed into the pub), and oceanic fayre such as wicked-looking shark teeth and a gigantic jawbone from one of the great whales. There were harpoons - long, brutal rods of iron with savage, jagged hooks at one end, and a host of giant cleavers and other vicious tools; someone around here had obviously done some whaling at one time.

Figgis returned to the alcove, carefully carrying the folio, and Quentin couldn't help but notice that the crowd had suddenly dimmed their rowdiness. They all seemed to be gazing on the folio, just as he found *himself* doing, and a silent reverence seemed to pass between them all.

"I offer it to you *gladly*," said Figgis in a quiet, somewhat *curious* manner, and bowed his head to Quentin. "Take your time, and it will give its story to you better that way."

Quentin found himself almost quivering with anticipation. With a 'clack' that seemed to echo throughout the hushed room, he opened the folio and examined the first page.

As before, as in his dreams, he felt his fingers caressing the sheets. The first page was one he recognised; a beautiful young girl, of about eight years of age. "This is Beathas," explained Figgis. "Her spirit dances with the hares on the hill at sunrise each morning."

Ignoring Figgis's mumbo-jumbo, Quentin tried to show

appreciation for what was obviously something of deep, Gaelic importance, but without being able to read the text beneath, he was struggling.

Figgis recognised this, and translated some of the words. It transpired she was born some some hundred and sixteen years ago, but glanced her head on a rock near the river and passed away from her injury.

Quentin bluntly responded with "But you said she 'dances with hares', or someth -."

"This is what we *believe*, Mr D'Orsey," interrupted Figgis, in a soothing tone.

So that was it then, thought Quentin, trying to grasp some sense of reason from it all. It's some kind of *mystical remembrance* book.

Figgis encouraged him to read on. There was a sheet about an elderly crofter named Tadhg; he'd died one hundred and forty-two years earlier, and Figgis assured Quentin his ghost could often be seen above the cairn of stones he'd been buried under. This continued for what could have been an hour or more, Figgis gently guiding Quentin as he studied, embraced, and *absorbed* every sheet. Despite his initial reservations to what he assumed Figgis saw as some kind of Gaelic tradition he found he couldn't help but be engrossed by the stories; these tales of fishermen, crofters, land-workers, children, mothers, wives - the stories of their lives and, perhaps more importantly, of their deaths.

He reached the penultimate page; a sheet depicting a young woman in her bridal gown. Quentin shivered, visibly; it filled him with anxiety as he knew the face that would be on the page that followed. But again Figgis's calming approach seemed to soothe him, and Quentin found himself forgetting about what might come, and examined the sheet in front of him instead.

It had a peculiar brownish stain in one corner, he noticed, that he took to be some imperfection in the parchment, or an ink blot.

There was faint, ever-so-delicate *stitching* also, as if the parchment had once had holes that needed to be repaired. "Aye, she had a fair complexion," said Figgis, "but it was always a shame about that lesion on her face."

Confused, D'Orsey looked at her illustration, and saw a large, blotted facial mark - identical in shape to the one on the sheet. He felt himself rubbing at the parchment; the thin, ridged holes that had been stitched felt almost like ... closed *eyelids*, and a *shrivelled mouth*. Realisation hit Quentin like a hammerblow then ... the sheets were made of human skin!

Revolted, D'Orsey tried to drop the folio and back away, but Figgis was quick to scoop them up and keep them in front of him. In a silent rush, several men from the main area of the bar came forward to pin Quentin down - and to his horror he saw in a flashing glimpse that *everyone* inside the pub wore identical animal masks to those from his dreams. Hare, fox, rodent, fish, insect - a heaving roomful of representations of nature's wildlife, and each with unblinking slits for eyes.

"Just the one sheet *remaining* now, Mr D'Orsey," said Figgis, all gentleness from his voice now gone.

"No!" the struggling Quentin roared in defiant response. "*No*, I say! I-I won't *do* it!"

Holding his hands in vice-like grips, two of the burliest mask-wearers forced his fingers to turn away the penultimate sheet, so he could view the last one.

"And *there you go* ..." said Figgis calmly, like a doting mother dispensing medicine to a child. Quentin tried to keep his eyes shut, but another of the mask-wearers grabbed at his face and forced his eyelids to open. And there, at last, in all its terror and majesty, was the page of the grim-faced man once more.

Quentin could hear Figgis talking to him again, explaining who the man was and *what* he was to his clan, but the nightmare was already beginning to manifest itself again once more and he found himself being lost inside it.

Quentin *screamed* as the piercing stare of the man burned at his eyes, and he choked in fear as he saw the sheet of skin beginning to ripple, as the mighty hands lifted up from the page and began to manifest in solid form. Once more they crawled in spider-like fashion up his neck and on to his face and head, and began to mercilessly paw and claw at his jaws.

And then all turned black for Quentin D'Orsey.

He woke in sporadic fits, catching fleeting glimpses of his surroundings. He was cold and no longer in the ale house, but had been bound and lain on wet turf, making him shiver. Quentin was surrounded by the masked villagers, their animal faces all flickering in the light of the fiery torches they carried. He felt a fresh breeze on his skin, and heard the roar of water; he was beside the river.

He could hear Figgis speaking, a boom above the sound of the cascading river nearby. No, not speaking; *chanting*. It sounded like some kind of prayer, or incantation. The rest of the throng repeated the words also, but in a quieter, more serene tone;

"Bidh èadhar agus grian, a 'dèanamh an sgòth,
Agus tha fios aig sgòth càite an tèid e.
Bidh Cloud a 'dèanamh uisge, stòr na beatha.
Agus bidh uisge a 'tòiseachadh air a thuras.

Aon drop an toiseach, an uairsin mòran a bharrachd.
An uairsin bidh uisge a 'fàs torrent,
Bidh sruthan a 'fàs na h-aibhne fiadhaich,
A 'gairm air a h-uile duine a chluinneas i."

As the words were spoken, D'Orsay noticed the waters of the river beginning to churn and bubble and froth, as if the brook was experiencing some fey, unaccountable *surge* coming down from its origins in the island's hills, or as if the waterway had suddenly become *alive* with a great many hundreds of fish. Sure enough; a salmon leaped up suddenly, slapping briefly against a rock on the side of the river. Then another, and another, until countless *thousands* were leaping and diving about the river in front of Figgis as he continued ...

"Abhainn a 'gairm an èisg bhig
Agus bidh iasg beag a 'fàs nas motha.
An uairsin bidh bradan a 'snàmh le toil suas an abhainn
Oir tha fios aige air an oidhirp aige.

Leig fios le làn ghealach dè an duine a bhios ag èigheach,
Leig le craobh seasamh gu làidir agus talamh a 'tighinn

Gaoth, uisge, teine agus uamh as dorcha
Agus chì iadsan a tha nan còmhnaidh a-staigh

Bidh iasg a 'sabaid an làn
Is e an Abhainn beatha, is sinne am bradan
'Bidh cnuimheag agus dubhan a 'tarraing èisg bho uisge
Agus bheir iasgair beatha bhuat."

Once Figgis had finished, the churning in the river slowly ceased and the waters returned to their previous state. A masked child slipped away from the clan and skipped up him. "Tha e na dhùisg," she whispered, giggling. *He is awake.*

Figgis walked toward Quentin. "Ah, awake *at last*, Mr D'Orsay. Glad to see you've come round well enough. I do hope you managed to see at least *some* of what the river had to show us all."

"What *is* all this?" spat D'Orsay, indicating the masked figures that surrounded them. "Some kind of *depraved ceremonial?*"

The assembled group all laughed. "Well, we don't see it that way," Figgis replied with a smile. "Call it 'a calling'."

"A calling to what?" growled Quentin.

"Not what; *who*," Figgis answered. "A calling to *Baran Fitheach*; the man in the folio - an elder of our clan, who passed some two hundred years gone. "And we all thank you for playing your part in his calling."

"I-I really don't understa-."

"Of course not," said Figgis. "How could you? Our ways are not yours. But we have called *Baran Fitheach*, and now he will come. He was a fisherman of this island, and then a whaler. Many would call him much, much worse, and perhaps not without justification. The folio belongs to *him*, Mr D'Orsey; it collects the souls of persons of our clan, or of those we merely wish to *add* to the collection. We take their skin upon their death and by enchanted bond their spirits remain tethered to it. Some souls are kept for good purpose; like living memories, if you will. But others have other purposes - they're more like *food*, you could say. *Baran Fitheach* saw more lands and learned more things than you or I could *ever* see, and that's how he came upon the folio. It was crafted in some Eastern land the outside world has yet to find. But for him to come we needed the right ... *fish*. And *you* were that fish, Mr D'Orsay."

Quentin was confused and aghast, and squirmed in his bonds angrily. "Y-you mean to say you went all that way ... *hundreds of miles,* from one end of the country to the other, acting the part of a sniveling fool, and - and - *ensnared me* with those ... those damnable pages of ... of *skin* ... just to get me back here for ... for *what*? Revenge? Is this what this is?"

"No, no; not revenge," Figgis answered calmly. "I was merely *the net* - cast wide to catch the right fish. You were chosen; your part in his calling has been played, as I have said. And now you can go, Mr D'Orsay."

At this, one of the villagers came forward and brusquely cut away Quentin's bonds. Numb and stiff, he rose awkwardly, even with assistance from two of the others.

Figgis picked out one of the villagers. "Colm here will take you back in his boat; dawn's not far off and you should be back on the mainland by mid-morning. You'll come to no harm with Colm, I can assure you."

"You mentioned you'd be taking up Bourne's offer," reminded Quentin warily, rubbing his wrists where he'd been bound and wondering to himself *how* he could think about work at a time like this. After all that had happened, he would much rather Figgis had said 'no' to the job; the man and his 'clan' were obviously all *utterly barking mad*, and he was just astounded these lunatics hadn't tried to boil him in a pot and eat him.

"And I *will* take up the offer," Figgis replied. "I'll be in touch with Mr Bourne in a day or two. But for now, why don't you put your feet up at your hotel. Grab a day off at the *Excelsior's* expense. Goodbye, Mr D'Orsey."

Quentin was led by Colm down to a rugged natural harbour, formed where the end of the river met the sea. There, a small fishing boat moored to a post bobbed in the moonlight. Amiably, Colm helped Quentin onboard and they set sail.

There was so much about the past day that made no sense to D'Orsey. He tried running the events over in his mind, and tried running questions past Colm as dawn arose. Unfortunately, Colm appeared to speak no word of English.

They made it to the ferry jetty by mid-morning as Figgis had promised, and Colm cheerily waved him off as he turned and headed back to the island. His mind reeling, Quentin kicked stones grumpily as he slowly made his way back to the hotel.

D'Orsey did as Figgis had suggested and spent the rest of the day at the hotel; first in the bar, then the dining hall, then the bar again. A couple of golfers, using the bar as their '19th hole', tried to raise a conversation out of him, but he wasn't interested.

Quentin had a quick nap late in the afternoon, followed by a walk down to the shingly beach to chuck stones into the sea. After half an hour of pebble chucking, he wearily shuffled back in the dining hall and bar again.

He finally called it a night around 11pm, when it was obvious the hotelier didn't keep the bar open after hours, and he returned to his room in a slightly wobbly manner after a final order of another treble whiskey.

After his hectic couple of days and the effects of fresh sea air and his nightcap, Quentin went off to sleep pretty quickly, snoring to high heaven and dreaming of soon getting back to his personal notion of civilisation.

He woke a couple of hours later; he'd neglected to shut his curtains, and the blinding radiance of the full moon was irritatingly high in a clear night sky above the island.

He didn't notice the silhouette against the window at first, until it moved, ever-so-slightly. A dark, hulking shape stood there, rising and falling with laboured breaths.

Forcing himself upright in his bed, Quentin went looking for a bedside light switch, only to find it didn't work once finally located.

"Who the devil's there?" D'Orsey barked.

"The devil *indeed*," came a slow, wet growl.

"How *dare* you get in this room - *whoever* you are," Quentin continued in his usual haughty manner. "What are you - so kind of *thief*?"

The shape seemed to ponder on this question for some time. "Thief ... *aye* ... that's about the truth of it," the silhouette eventually replied. It was a languid, laconic, disconcerting rumble of a voice; there was no hurry to its menace.

The shape moved closer a step, a heavy, water-laden boot squelching on to the ground. Then another.

"My name is Baran Fitheach, *Little Fish*," it rasped, "and I'm here for you at last, boy."

At that, Quentin yelped and jumped out of his bed, but his foot caught fast in his sheets and he fell in a tangled heap on to the floor. He screamed and screamed as loud as his lungs would let him, and began thumping on the floor in an attempt to get somebody's attention.

"No-one can *hear you*, Little Fish," the silhouette growled. The voice was thick with the sound of oozing moisture, like the slop of saturated mud under foot. "Just you and me now."

Quentin felt his heart hammering in his chest, beating so fast he feared it would give out. *Still* he tried to get away but the shape was on him now; long, slick hair dripping with briny water dragged like seaweed across Quentin's face as the shape stood over him. The rancid stench of the rotting things that die and fall to the bottom of the sea poured like a torrent from the figure's mouth, while tortuous, rasping breaths from its saturated lungs made the room shudder with their deep rumble.

There was a heavy *thump* and the shape dropped an enormous sack on to the floor from its shoulder. The contents seemed to *writhe* and *shift* as it settled on the ground.

And then the strong hands came, pawing at D'Orsey's

neck and face; one settling on his forehead and the other on his jaw. With inhuman strength the figure pulled the mouth apart, wrenching and twisting until with a sickening *snap* there came the crack of bone, Quentin screaming all the while.

The hulking shape hummed to itself while it worked; some ancient sea shanty it had picked up on a storm-wracked ocean journey it had once made, so many years ago. It dug its hands deep into the sack and began to thrust the contents down D'Orsey's throat, the definition of the writhing, wriggling shapes becoming evident to him now that his life was almost ended.

Salmon. They were salmon.

The thing continued its hellish work, way, way beyond when Quentin D'Orsey's life had ceased to be. In the morning, the hotelier would find a distorted, colossal lump of human flesh *crammed* with hundreds of dead fish, and the little town of Droichead Cloiche would have an unfathomable mystery to decipher. First though, the grim-faced shape that was Baran Fitheach had its work to finish. When no fish remained, Fitheach dug deep into the sack and retrieved a long iron rod, with a twist of metal at one end. As Fitheach mumbled some indecipherable words the tip ignited and glowed a fiery red, before he rammed it hard into what had once been Quentin's forehead, and left the burning brandmark of a fish.

The final task was to remove a section of skin, that would be stretched, then hung out to tan and dry. One day it would be another sheet in Baran Fitheach's folio - it would be inked with the details of D'Orsey's life and death, and added to all the others in his collection. The dark figure rummaged in the deep, slime-and-filth-filled pockets of its shapeless overcoat until grimy fingers came upon a rusted skinning knife. Choosing a smooth section of skin that had once covered Quentin's back, Fitheach cut and peeled until he had what he needed.

"Now ... that's the meat work done, but I want your *soul*," the dark shape growled as it slowly made its made out of the bedroom. "I'll be becoming back for you *tomorrow*, boy. Don't you be going anywhere."

There were only two living souls in the room when Baran Fitheach returned the next evening - a constable on watch named Jack Fraser and Saoirse Preston, a forensics officer. Neither noticed the apparition as it entered, just as they'd been unaware all day of Quentin's spirit, which was now cowering and desperately pleading atop the wardrobe where'd he'd been recalling his final days.

Gone was the sack and the branding iron - Fitheach this time carried a long, steel hook in one hand, and dragged a heavy fisherman's net with the other. With a cruel smile playing across what had once been a mouth, the apparition slowly approached the wardrobe.

The dark spirit pointed up at D'Orsay's ghost with his hook, then made a pulling motion - in response, the ghost of Quentin D'Orsey flew from his spot atop the wardrobe and landed at Fitheach's feet. Growling, the dark fisherman buried the hook *deep* through both of Quentin's cheeks; a salmon being caught on a fishing hook. "Caught ye at last, Little Fish," the spirit growled, then reached down and pressed his palm on Quentin's forehead, making the brand mark of the salmon burn white hot on his skin and leaving D'Orsay's phantom kicking and screaming in wretched agony. The fishing net dropped heavily to the floor, and Fitheach began to hoist D'Orsay into it. He would pull Quentin's soul back across the expanse of sea to Creag Dhubh island, and then down to the river, where the spirits of his clan could feed on his soul for eternity. Laughing darkly to himself, Baran Fitheach bundled Quentin D'Orsey's ghost into his net and began dragging him away.

Saoirse Preston felt a cold, clammy shiver down her spine as the two spirits passed through her on the way out. It wasn't the first time she'd felt similar; a disadvantage, she supposed, of working with the dead. Stretching and straightening her collar, she shrugged the feeling off and returned to her forensics work.

"Mr Bourne, this is Alexander Figgis. *Hello*, very pleasant to speak to you at long last. Yes ... I'm feeling much better, thank you. Mr Bourne; I'm obviously calling in regard to the employment situation with the *Excelsior*, but I'm afraid there's another matter - Mr D'Orsey appears to have suffered some horrendous accident at his hotel. Indeed ... it's all rather *dreadful*. I'm not sure of the facts at this stage, but as I'm in the vicinity, would you like me to cover the story for you?"

THE END

HE WHO PLAYS THE DEVIL'S TUNE

Travis Benton was a musician, of the 'struggling' variety. His ambition, like many others of his ilk, had once been to be a guitarist in a rock and roll band. Unfortunately for Travis, the closest he ever got to such a lifestyle was hauling around sound and stage equipment for *other* musicians.

It was a job he certainly didn't hate and was, as they say, 'in the blood' (his father had been a roadie, years earlier) - but, as I'm sure you can appreciate, it wasn't quite the same as getting up on stage and doing it for yourself.

In recent months he'd been touring around the country with a band called *Byron's Rejected*. All in all, he'd found them 'pretty cool'; he got to hang out with the band on the tour bus, got to tune-up guitars for the musicians before they performed on stage, and even got the chance to jam with them from time to time during rehearsals. But it wasn't, as I said, quite the same.

However, they'd reached the last night of the tour and - stroke of luck - the Astoria Theatre they were playing in was less than a mile from his flat. He'd have several months of unpaid bills to wade through once he'd finally got the flat's front door open and it'd be freezing inside (what with the power being off for so long) - but he'd be in his own bed for the first time in ages, and that sounded like utter bliss.

The band played, the crowd lapped it up. It was a great gig; one of the best of the tour. *Byron's Rejected* were really taking off and it was more than likely there'd be more touring work for Travis next year.

Once everyone began to shuffle out, it was just down to Travis and the handful of other road crew to pack up the gear in the van and then he could call it a night. Then it was just a matter of a quick trip to Amal's Kebab Shop and the late night off licence on the way home and he'd be sorted out for the evening. Humming one of the band's tunes to himself, he disconnected the lead guitarist's amp, lifted it and made to head toward the stage exit. And it was at this point in Travis Benton's life that things began to, shall we say, veer off in directions unexpected ...

Standing directly in front of him was what Travis instantly recognised to be a ghost. I suppose if one is confronted with a supernatural apparition there is usually a degree of uncertainty in regards to what one is actually looking at, but in Travis's situation there could be no doubt in his mind.

Here was a translucent figure of a man, about six feet in height, who wore 'distinctive' clothing Travis would describe as retro, historical or downright old-fashioned, from (by his estimation) the nineteen sixties or seventies period. The ghost wore a cuffed, 'bohemian' shirt, billowing and open to the navel, flared satin pants and tall platform-heeled boots. In addition, the figure wore a runic-symbolled bandana in black, and very long hair that fell well beyond his shoulders. Travis would perhaps describe his tanned physique as 'slim and predatorial' - with his arrogant posture, this spectre looked every inch the 'Rock God', and this spectre knew it. And naturally he had dark, piercing eyes and a ridiculously handsome face to top it all off.

But the one thing that stood out above all else was the very large silver 'pentangle' medallion about the ghost's neck, which appeared to pulsate and emanate a sickly yellow glow. Travis struggled to take his gaze away from it - it was so alluring, and seemed to hold the promise to so many things, if he would only reach out and take it for himself.

Although Travis instantly saw (or perhaps 'felt' is a better word) that this definitely *was* a ghost, it took his mind a little while to register that all was perhaps 'not well' and that he should perhaps react accordingly. This he soon did, clumsily dropping the hefty amp he'd been holding, and stumbling backwards over other stage equipment that had yet to be removed.

The spell of the pendant broken, he raced toward the opposite wing of the stage. A belated wail escaped from Travis, which made another roadie - an ancient Cornishman named Jasper - look up from the mess of tangled cables he was trying to unknot and try to see what all the fuss was about.

"Hey, you alright, boy?" called Jasper, grabbing him by the arm as he whizzed past. "Look like you've seen a ghost."

"Wha-? I-I think I just *have*," Travis replied, shakily. "J-just then - it *w-was* a ghost, or something I ..."

"Now what do you *mean*, exactly?" Jasper slowly answered, calming Travis down with his laconic style, but eyeing the younger roadie with genuine concern.

Travis continued to stammer. "Back … back there … o-on the stage just then. I'm sure I …" He dared a look back toward the stage. Only a cluster of abandoned stage equipment remained. No ghost.

"Just take your time, lad," the old roadie interjected. "No need to rush things." He pointed to a couple of chairs in the wings of the stage, and encouraged him to sit down. "Okay. Deep breaths. And start from the top, eh?"

Travis rested for a minute, composing himself, and told his tale. Once he'd finished, the older man had an answer for him.

"Ahh, now I reckon that'll be the ghost of *Dominic Ravenstone* you saw," Jasper drawled with a wry smile. He casually lit up a roll-up, ignoring all the fire hazard warning signs plastered everywhere.

"Dominic Ravenstone?" Travis responded in bemusement. "Who the hell's Dominic Ravenstone?"

Jasper laughed a little, his leathery features illuminated by the flickering light from his smoke.

"Your dad knew him," he said, by way of explanation. "Me too. We both toured with him, around sixty-eight, sixty-nine, or thereabouts. Him and Crazy Mary played together for a couple of years before that. Thankfully, me and your dad both got the boot when he formed a band called the Dark Spiritz."

"How do you mean, *thankfully*?" Travis asked.

"Because if we didn't then we'd probably both be dead a year later," the ancient roadie replied, with a grim chuckle. He looked around at the theatre. "This whole place went up in smoke, see; Dominic died, the audience died - *everyone* died. Couldn't get out, they reckon, but strangely enough there were no locked doors when the fire engines arrived. *No-one Leaves Alive*; that was the name of their album. Appropriate, when you think about it."

He took a long draw on his roll-up, and offered it to Travis, who shakily refused. With a shrug, Jasper continued. "But that's not the half of it, but any means. The only bandmember that died that night was Dominic, but the rest of the band all died days earlier."

Goggle-eyed, he waved his arms in a mock-mystical fashion and cackled the laugh of a man who should have given up smoking twenty years earlier.

"They were all into that devil-worshipping stuff; all the 'heavy' bands were, at the time. It were part of the image, see? And if you ask me, I reckon that's what did for them in the end. And as for you seeing Dominic's ghost ... well, let's just say you ain't been the first to see such things over the years."

As you can probably imagine, at this point Travis wasn't exactly sure *what* to believe. He'd seen *something*, that was for certain - but he wasn't going to take old Jasper's wind-ups and urban myth stories at face value.

Travis stood up. "I-I think I'm gonna knock off early," he said, wearily. "Can you cover for me? I think I need an early night. Clear my head, or something."

Jasper gave him a 'thumbs up'.

"Aye, you do that," Jasper called after him as the younger roadie wandered off to the theatre exit, "but don't you go digging up things best left alone, lad." Out of earshot, Jasper mumbled to himself. "You don't wanna end up like those other poor beggars."

Appetite gone, Travis wandered past Amal's Kebab Shop and the off licence without stopping, the image of the apparition still fresh in his mind and the relentless, soaking rain beating down on his head a distant sensation. Finally, the worn blue paint of his flat's front door came into view, its tinge a murky green under the flickering sodium light. Travis delved into his pocket for his flat key and heaved against the pile of amassed mail that had stockpiled against the door.

Once inside he made straight for his bed.

He woke suddenly at three a.m., and had that unnerving, nape-of-the-neck feeling that he was being watched. Like any rational person who wakes up three a.m. with such feelings, it took Travis a considerable amount of time to fearfully open his eyes, peer over the sheets and convince himself that it was just his imagination. Unfortunately for Travis, this was one occasion when he probably shouldn't have.

Standing at the foot of his bed was the ghost of Dominic Ravenstone. His piercing eyes buried themselves in Travis's mind, the pentagram amulet bathing the room in its sickly aura. Gasping, Travis gathered his bedsheets around him and backed up against the wall.

"Wh-What the hell do you *want*?" he managed to yell at the spirit. "Just - just *leave me alone*, alright?!" In a panic he looked around for something to hurl at the apparition, and found his alarm clock. He threw it and the spectre immediately dissolved from view, with the last of the amber glow from the pendant fading as the clock thumped against the far wall.

Travis felt himself slowly relaxing as the uncanny presence vanished. Outside, he could hear the rain continuing to pour against his bedroom window and the swirling sound of rainwater gurgling down the drainpipe. He remained pressed up against the bedroom wall with his sheets for the rest of the night, only realising he'd eventually fallen asleep when dawn's light woke him once more.

After a breakfast of stale cereal and dubiously still-in-date long life milk, Travis decided he'd have to get some information on Dominic Ravenstone and the Dark Spiritz. Fortunately, he knew he wouldn't have to look far. On the same street as Travis's flat stood Big Peggy's Sounds; a small, independent music store that was (as you may have guessed) run by a large lady named Peggy.

When it came to getting info on long-forgotten heavy rockers, she would be the perfect person to speak to. As well as having one of the finest encyclopaedic brains in the country when it came to rock music, Peggy was also of the 'gothic rock' persuasion; black lipstick, shaved eyebrows, multiple piercings and ninety per cent of her body covered in tattoos of skulls, bats, winged demons and pentagram symbols. Unsurprisingly, Travis shivered at the thought of pentagrams.

The only issue was Travis found her utterly terrifying to deal with; it wasn't just her appearance that he found formidable; Peggy basically saw her customers as 'utter scum', and tended to treat them as such - after all, she was there to sell records to people, not treat them as humans, and she was likely to (literally) throw customers out the door if she took a meaner than usual dislike to anyone.

Steeling himself for the visit after a shower, Travis made the short trip down the street to her store. It was *still* pouring with rain, and by the time he reached the shop he'd wondered why he'd bothered with the shower. Timorously, he walked inside and was immediately hit by a wall of sound from the shop's stereo speakers; some ominous, Eastern European industrial dirge that Travis (or indeed anyone except Peggy) would struggle to call music.

And there she was, at the far end of the shop; Big Peggy. A gargantuan sentinel behind the counter, her unblinking eyes on Travis the moment he'd crossed the threshold. Naturally there were no other customers that morning, which meant he got her undivided attention. Travis felt himself sweating nervously; this was ridiculous, he chided himself - he was a *grown man*, for goodness sake. He nodded in her direction, a weak "Y'okay, Peggy?" escaping his lips. Ominously, he got no response. Just those cold, unblinking eyes.

Trying to ignore her laser stare, he made toward the D section of the store, and began rifling through the albums on sale. Nothing there, in regards to Dominic Ravenstone. He moved to the R section instead, to try looking under surnames; after a minute of flicking through the albums on sale he found what he was looking for, stuffed away at the back and covered in a thick layer of dust; *No-one Leaves Alive* by Dominic Ravenstone and the Dark Spiritz, recorded 1970.

A bellow cut through the air, so loud the industrial grind

from the stereo sounded like a whisper in comparison. With his nervous disposition being somewhat fragile at the moment, it made Travis almost drop the album in shock.

"Y'buying that, or what?!" Peggy roared.

Head down fearfully, he scurried toward the sales counter; it was best to get this over with, he reasoned to himself. Travis handed the album over and rummaged in his pocket for the necessary cash. Once he'd placed the money on the counter he found Peggy's eyes passing between the album and himself; it was as if she were judging whether he was *suitable-enough* to listen to it.

"Any chance of a carrier bag?" he shouted over the cacophony, partially in an attempt to get a conversation flowing, and partially because he didn't want the rain outside to turn the record's ancient sleeve to pulp. With a glare, Peggy reached under the counter and produced a carrier bag as requested.

"Know anything about them?" Travis shouted again, nodding at the album. No response. He tried again. There was a very long pause.

Sighing, Peggy shifted her bulk toward the stereo's volume, and turned it down. Oh, she had a talker. Great.

"Of course I know about them," she replied in a deadpan drone. "And as you're paying for it I suppose you now want some background information. Dominic Ravenstone on vocals. Stumpy Moncreiff on lead guitar. Chipper Harris, bass guitar. Nobby Greenhalf on keyboards and Harry 'The Governor' Phipps on drums."

"And all dead within a week or two of releasing the album, so I'm told," shrugged Travis, in a manner which said 'please tell me more'.

Peggy looked beyond this lowlife time waster. Zero customers in her shop. Again. What was the matter with people these days - didn't they like music? Oh, what the hell ... Her monotone resumed, and turned into a monologue. "Harry 'The Governor' Phipps died in a bizarre car crash on Maida Vale Road; new brickwork can still be seen under the railway bridge where his car - a forest green Morris Minor - ploughed into the wall at high speed. His separated body parts (and there were many) were located up to three hundred yards away. Nobody knows why. Moving on to Nobby Greenhalf; he was seemingly mauled to death and half eaten by wild animals within his own flat - though the door was locked from the inside, there was no evidence of forced entry, no wild animals at the scene and no noises had been heard by his neighbours. A curious case, as I'm sure you will agree. A similar death befell Chipper Harris; he was also found half-eaten in his apartment, except this time there were no claw marks. It appears he developed a taste for his own flesh, and decided to keeping on eating his own body parts until his vital functions gave out. Stumpy Moncreiff meanwhile, was, for reasons unknown, found skinned alive and nailed to the ceiling of a disused church. Again, a curious case indeed. And that just leaves Dominic Ravenstone."

There was a very lengthy pause, before Travis couldn't stand the wait any longer and interrupted it with a near-desperate "Yes?! What about him?"

Peggy continued, unblinking. "Once his bandmembers had all promptly died, Ravenstone tried to tour with session musicians, to promote the album. Unfortunately, on the very first night of the tour, the theatre he was performing at burnt down with everyone inside - Ravenstone, the musicians, the staff and the crowd - all dying a slow and painful death."

"That'll be the Astoria," said Travis.

"Well, if you know everything, what are you asking *me* for?" grunted Peggy, and snapped his money off the counter. She made to go back to the volume control on the stereo, but Travis stopped her with a question.

"One last thing," he began, before struggling to find the right words. "All these deaths ... they're horrific. Why ... why don't people know more about all this? I mean - this is up there with some of the weirdest deaths that've happened in the history of rock music, wouldn't you say?"

"*Dead news*, innit?" she shrugged, and cranked up the volume.

A quick pit stop at the local convenience store for food supplies, then Travis returned to his flat to listen to the album. After grabbing a beer, he sat down to peruse the album's artwork.

There was Dominic Ravenstone alright, with an arrogant hands-on-hips posture and looking exactly like the spectre he'd twice seen the night before - complete with shining pentangle pendant on a heavy chain around his neck. On the cover photo, he and the other band members were arranged standing at the five points of a pentagram that had been painted on the floor. Ravenstone was in the foreground, while a pair of slim guitarists (who were presumably Stumpy Moncreiff and Chipper Harris) stood on either side. Making up the two final points of the inverted star were Nobby Greenhalf standing at his keyboards and Harry 'The Governor' Phipps with his drums. While Ravenstone had gone for the strutting 'Rock God' look previously mentioned, Moncreiff had Harris had painted their faces a skull-like white and black, and wore lengthy smocks covered in astrological symbols. Nobby Greenhalf had gone for the *Hammer Horror* look, wearing a frankly ludicrous Frankenstein-type face mask, claws and a frilly shirt, while Harry 'The Governor' Phipps, showing some restraint, simply wore a pair of unrealistic horns and a velvet suit.

"Ridiculous," chuckled Travis who felt, now that he'd seen them all in the cold light of day, that there perhaps wasn't quite so much to be concerned about in regards to this bunch of rock dinosaurs. He flipped the sleeve over, and saw another group shot of the band.

This time they were all grouped together, raising their hands at the camera in a claw-like manner and flashing pairs of fake vampire teeth while fake blood trickled down their mouths and chins. "Hmm, terrifying," said Travis to himself and shaking his head, "hopefully the music won't be as cheesy - though I'm not holding out much hope."

He scanned the titles of the ten songs listed on the reverse sleeve, and the song credits. Side One: *No-one Leaves Alive, Trainwreck to Damnation, Blood of My Beauty, The Devil's Calling, Zombie Blues.* Side Two: *Hellriders, The Cursed Moon, Prayer to the Old Gods, Sweet Sacrifice, No-one Leaves Alive (Part II).* Most of the songs, he noticed, were written by Dominic Ravenstone and someone called Crazy Mary - now, *where* had he heard that name before? It came to him eventually; old Jasper had briefly mentioned her back at the theatre. There'd been no mention by Peggy of anyone called Crazy Mary meeting a hideous fate like all the others, though.

"Well, time to give it a whirl," Travis said to himself, and popped the disk on to his record player's turntable.

Whatever had been the reason for the ghostly Dominic Ravenstone's appearance, Travis soon surmised it was at least in part to do with him listening to this album. From the moment the first guitar note played he realised he'd been ensnared. He sat transfixed, rooted to the spot, unable to move as every lyric and line of music conjured daemonic visions of hellish greed and death and lust and power. His mundane bedroom faded away to reveal a ghostly plain shrouded in mist, where unseen shapes caused twisting vortices in the miasma and that same nauseous yellow light oozed across the landscape. At times he'd feel himself being dragged and pulled downward into the cloying aether by grasping hands, while screeching bat-things and skull-faced monstrosities flew about his head and clawed at his hair and eyes. He tried to scream, but the smothering mist choked every cry.

Beneath the music were layer after layer of chants and incantations, all summoning him, urging him, *leading* him forward step after agonising step across the plain until eventually, finally, the source of the yellow light revealed itself. A theatrical stage appeared, on to which a five star pentagram had been painted. At each point of the star stood one of the musicians; a living facsimile of the album sleeve, their eyes burned into him like coals. Dominic Ravenstone leered menacingly at the foremost point, his pentangle medallion burning Travis's vision with its amber radiance.

"All earthly pleasures can be yours," boomed Ravenstone's voice like thunder. "Success, power ... whatever your desires. Just offer yourself without reserve and take the amulet."

Travis found himself on the stage a moment later, Ravenstone and the pendant a mere arm's reach away.

"*Take it*, boy," Ravenstone gasped and sighed, as if in joyful expectation of the freedom he would feel once the amulet had been taken from him. "It can all be yoursss ..." The malevolent spirit smiled in cruel satisfaction as Travis felt his right hand reaching out, fingers like putty as they delicately moved toward the pendant. Images of ambition, power and success swirled within his mind - no longer would he need to be a lackey to others; soon *the world* would praise his music. Just reach out and take it ...

He stopped. His reached no further. Something, somewhere from the deepest recesses of his brain told him this was wrong. All wrong.

He gained some clarity of mind. Inches away, the face of Dominic Ravenstone glared at him with unreserved hatred, the fiery pits of his eyes burning in his own. "*Take it*, boy!"

Travis backed away, shaking his head. "No!" he managed to shout. "Noooo!" A deafening, screeching chorus rose up around him as Travis got further away, turning about himself in desperation to find some way out of this hell. With a final booming thundercrack and blinding flash he was knocked from his feet, and drifted into unconsciousness.

When he awoke it was the middle of the night once more.

He found himself alone and sprawled across the stage floor of the Astoria.

The following morning, Big Peggy saw Travis making a beeline for her counter and the sound of her East European industrial dirge-music only just managed to make her curses and swearing inaudible.

"Thirty quid!" she bellowed at him before he'd had chance to say anything. "You want any more information, it'll cost yer thirty quid."

Grumbling, Travis turned on his heel, went to the cash machine on the other side of the street, and returned with the necessary funds. Once she saw the funds she turned down the music's volume a little.

"I suppose you want to know about Crazy Mary Mulcahy," she said, swiftly scooping up the cash. Travis nodded. He'd concluded years earlier that all women were psychic and Peggy was obviously no exception.

"*Eventually*," he replied. "First, I'd like you to tell me some more about that album - and where the hell you got it from."

Peggy didn't like the somewhat *crazed look* in this punter's eye. She'd known just by looking at him that he wasn't cut out for heavy rock. "I got that album from the dealers, like all my other stock. My dad Bill sorts it out so you better not have any complaints. And I've listened to it myself, once or twice. It's not bad, actually."

Travis really, *really* wanted to ask if it had transferred her to some kind of demonic universe and tried to take her soul, but somehow he found the will to keep that one bottled down. "Okay," he said eventually. "Just tell me about Crazy Mary."

Peggy went into monologue mode once more. "Crazy Mary got kicked out of the band, on account of her not being into all the satanic stuff they started messing around in. Being a woman probably didn't help her either, as men were sexist bastards in those days. Still are. But she was far and away the best musician to ever work with Ravenstone, and half of the songs on that album you bought were written by her, as you've probably noticed if you've read the song credits."

Travis was dreading asking the next question. "So ... just supposing there was ... some kind of curse on the band, or some kind of satanic pact ... some supernatural reason why they all died so horribly ... does that mean she fell foul of it too?"

The constant deadpan (some would say lifeless) expression on Peggy's face gave nothing away in regards to what she thought of him or that particular question.

"Mary Mulcahy lives in Wimbledon," she replied, flatly. "She's turned her house into a care home for cats, like most mad ex-hippies and failed rockers do. So no, I don't think she fell foul of some kind of satanic pact; only an idiot *would*."

Back at his flat, it didn't take Travis too long to hunt Mary down; a quick flick through the Yellow Pages listed three cat sanctuary style organisations in the Wimbledon area, and hers was the second he rang. She picked up the phone herself; he was greeted by her soft Irish accent and lots of cat meows in the background.

A 'vague' explanation on the phone secured a meeting with her the following day; assuring her he wasn't some kind of reporter or investigator, Travis said he'd come across the album, and just wanted to chat with her about it. He also mentioned his dad had known her when he'd been a roadie, and that they had a mutual acquaintance in old Jasper.

There'd been some reluctance in her voice, he noticed that much, at which Travis had little surprise. But she'd promised she'd talk to him, and that felt like a lifeline for now. Little to do then, but try and forget about things until the meeting. And not play that bloody album ever again. Not wanting to look at the thing, he picked up the disk from his turntable, placed it and the sleeve in a black binbag and dumped everything into the dustbin outside.

At three a.m. Travis found himself awake once more. Slowly rising from his bed, he went to the bedroom window, to look down on the street below; his shuffling feet moving without instruction, his mind and body unable to resist. Pollution and dirt had grimed into a thick veneer on the glass outside. How long had it been since he'd had the windows cleaned; a year? Never? The perpetual rain made the illumination from the road lamps and car headlights warp and melt like an oil painting doused in white spirit, and the drains beneath his window rattled with their worn-out overuse.

But there ... *there*, directly under the street lamp beneath his flat; there was that sickly yellow glow again - and despite the muck on his window pane and the relentless rain and darkness he could make out that same pentagram medallion as it burned like hot coals deep, *deep* into his mind. And from the black silhouette of the apparition bathing in the sodium lamplight radiance *two eyes* began to glow with the same sickly luminescence, urging him, *compelling* him on to some unspoken task or duty he knew he must fulfil.

He woke with a start hours later, his body sprawled awkwardly across the top of sweated, mangled bedsheets on his mattress.

Feeling as though he hadn't slept in a week, the temptation was to crawl back under the sheets; partly to sleep, partly to *hide*. Instead, cursing and grumbling aloud, he forced himself up and headed for the shower.

When Mary Mulcahy eventually met the shaking, distressed young man at her home's cat-clawed front door she could tell there was a lot more to this young man's request for a chat about the old days. Gently guiding Travis inside (and shooing away half a dozen of her curious felines), she sat him down in her living room and made them both a brew.

After a little light talk she approached the matter in hand. "Right, Travis; I'm going to tell you all I know. You stop me at any point if you need to ask anything. You stop me at any point if *you* need to tell *me* anything. There's a great deal of tragedy surrounding that record, and Lord knows I'd rather not remind myself of it - but I can see you've been *touched* by all this in some way, and certainly not for the better. So here goes ..." She took a final slurp of milky tea, then began.

"Dominic - or *Chunky* as I knew him - was a great guy, when first we met. That'd be around sixty-six to sixty-seven;

Summer of Love, and all that. We'd tour in his broken-down camper van, playing gigs in pubs and writing songs; nothing too major - just for fun, really. A bit of LSD, a bit of cannabis, but never anything out of control. *Chunky Fabb and Crazy Mary* we were known as," she laughed, her eyes distant in reminiscence. "And before you ask, he was called Chunky on account of his weight, and I was Crazy Mary on account of my antics; I was a bit of a wildchild, back in the day, and he could have afforded to lose a stone or two."

She chuckled a little, then began to frown. "Then he met one or two of the other guys; Chipper Harris and Nobby Greenhalf first, I think it was. They started getting bigger ideas, wanting to turn it all into some big money-making deal. It all seemed okay at first ... then, somewhere along the line they started messing about with all this ... *darker* stuff. First it was the heavier drugs, and I think all that God awful Charlie Manson stuff on the news was appealing to them. And Chunky was reading all this satanic stuff; books about witchcraft and black rites and what have you, and strutting around with a huge pentangle medallion around his neck. He said he picked it up from some flea market in Camden Lock, but I dunno. Anyhow, he lost a huge amount of weight in such a short time - and kept going on about changing his name, his image - everything. And before I knew it he was 'Dominic Ravenstone, Rock-God-in-waiting'. But, somehow, I dunno .. all of a sudden it all seemed to be *working out* for him; whatever he wanted, he seemed to get. *Anything*. Out of the blue he got a good record deal, and the company wanted him to have a name for the band, so they became the Dark Spiritz - and it wasn't long after that I got kicked out the band."

"But didn't you write most of the stuff on the album?" asked Travis.

"I did, aye," she responded with something akin to a malcontented growl, "but all my songs were *corrupted* with their darker lyrics and gloomy bass lines and creepy keyboard sounds. I couldn't *believe* the album when I finally got round to listening to it. Still, I got my percentage of the royalties - not much, but living was cheap in those days. But then the worst of it came, with all those grisly deaths and the fire and all, and I just wanted to get away from the whole thing."

"I wanted to ask about all that," interjected Travis, "but wasn't sure if -."

"Ah, it's okay," she responded with a shudder. "But it *was* awful. The papers were making a big song and dance about it all for a few weeks - which obviously helped the record company sell more copies - but it was all so gruesome I stopped reading about it in the end. Then Vietnam seemed to be grabbing all the headlines again, and it all kinda got forgotten about." Mary crossed herself, as if in memory of those who had died, then sighed.

One of Mary's cats suddenly jumped on her lap, demanding love and attention. She stroked it and the cat purred affectionally in response. It was a shabby old thing, Travis thought; one eye missing and ears torn to pieces - it'd obviously had a rough life. "Eventually I got round to setting up this place," she continued. "Saving souls like this wee fellah; that's my mission now."

Travis couldn't wait any longer, and asked her the question he really wanted to ask. "Look; this is going to sound completely nuts ... but I think there's some sort of curse on that band, or that album. Some kind of ... oh, I don't know, *malign influence*, shall we say." Travis laughed awkwardly. "Crazy, I know ..."

Mary thought for a long moment, considering everything. "No, Travis - I don't think that's crazy at all." Unconsciously, she reached for the crucifix necklace under her shirt before continuing. "If you let good things into your life, good things happen. If you let in *bad* ... well."

"I've been getting ... *visions*, Mary," Travis continued, and the wracked look of fear and anxiety on his features wasn't missed by the older woman. "It's Ravenstone again, I know it is. He *wants* something. Or at least, that pentangle medallion does. I keep seeing it. *And* him. Visions, dreams ... hallucinations. In my flat ... in the street. He's there, you know? Standing, waiting. All ominous and threatening. I-I don't know what it's all about, but ..."

"You need to get away from all this," she answered, firmly. "*Right now*. Is there anyone you can stay with? Your dad, perhaps?"

Travis shook his head. "He died eight years ago, Mary. Not long after mum."

Mary reached out for his hands, consoling him. "Oh, I'm so sorry, Travis - I never realised. Oh, you've had a time, haven't you? I knew your dad, for a while, as you know; he was a good man."

Awkwardness and embarrassment overcame Travis then, and rationality swept in. He'd offloaded his paranoia and these absurdities on a *complete stranger* and now he just wanted to leave. Maybe seeing his doctor would be a better idea.

"I-I'm sorry," he said, standing up. "I've made a complete fool of myself, haven't I? It's just stress, I suppose. I should go." Mary tried to convince him otherwise but he was soon at the front door and looking for the latch.

"Just promise me you'll look after yourself," she said with a sigh. "*Burn* that bloody record if you haven't already, get some rest and God go with you. Nothing good ever came of those final days with the band and I believe you when you say there's something *evil* about all this. I've got your number, you've got mine - and you know where I am if you want to talk some more."

Travis had another visitation that evening; the black silhouette once again standing silently beneath the street lamp close to his flat, and that sickly yellow glow.

In his weakness, Travis found he was unable to resist in any way this time; he found his body rising like an automaton from his bed and wandering to the window, and felt the piercing gaze from the apparition.

Travis stood unblinking, as it gave him an instruction.

The following morning, Travis left his flat around nine and headed toward the railway station. Once there, he purchased the necessary tickets he would need for his journey, and took the first of two connecting trains to Chichester.

Travis was only vaguely aware of his actions; the instructions he had received the night before had left him as little more than an unthinking zombie, fulfilling the orders he had received.

He arrived in Chichester, and took a cab to a destination on the very outskirts of the suburbs. For discretionary reasons, it appeared he had to *walk* the remainder of the journey, and he began a long hike along a number of country paths.

He eventually came to a pair of towering black gates - overgrown with vines as thick as branches, and slowly rusting to oblivion in their disrepair. Using all his strength he managed to push one ajar slightly, squeeze between the gap he'd forced so he could continue on his way.

Travis was soon stumbling along a stretch of private road, that snaked through what had once been a stretch of coppice woodland but had now become something closer to a wild and untamed forest. Branches overhung and coarse bush invaded the pathway, cutting at his arms and legs as the pressed onward.

The overgrown road eventually straightened, and led toward a decrepit manor house; a grim, uncared-for slab of Elizabethan bricks, with brooding clouds scudding across a monochrome sky above. Bleak, furrowed fields on either side of the road were peppered with carping ravens, while a withered ash tree gutted by a lightning strike sat lop-sided near the manor's entrance. The landscape had been used for farming once - agriculture of some kind - but was now no more than a hard, unworkable plain of ruts and coarse, twisted weeds.

A surreal, almost ritualistic scene waited for Travis in front of the house's immense oak doors. Here was a shrivelled old woman, her proportions tiny in comparison to the building behind her, her translucent skin-and-bone appearance so withered she appeared almost skeletal. To her left a black dog with pinned back ears and bared teeth snarled at him relentlessly with the barest of self-restraint.

To the frail woman's right a small wooden chest had been placed centrally on a slender, antique table. An ornate silver dagger had been rested on top of the chest, as had a silver goblet and white handkerchief.

A metre or so in front of this withered husk of a woman Travis felt himself coming to a stop, and, grasping a silver-capped waking cane, she slowly approached him.

Whereas Mary had exuded warmth and kindness, what remained of Travis's conscious mind felt nothing but coldness and loathing from this woman. A pair of severe, unblinking black eyes studied him, and reaching up she roughly *played* with the meat of his face, her withered hands so like the claws of the ravens that apathetically watched proceedings from the ruined old ash tree close by.

"Oh, we *are* in a bad way, aren't we, dear?" she mocked, the woman's grating voice like sandpaper on stone. "All alone out here and with no one to help you."

She leaned forward so her long, aquiline nose almost touched his, and peered with curiosity into his eyes. "I *know* you're still in there, begging to be set free ... but *I'm sorry*, my dear; there has to be 'an exchange'. There are much greater needs than yours at play at the moment."

The ancient woman continued. "My name is Lucretia Ravenstone, and the silver pendant you're familiar with has, you could say, been a *family heirloom* for quite some time. It's something of a *soul eater*, and I'm afraid it's rather ravenous once more."

Turning away slightly, she made her way to the table. Carefully placing her cane at rest beside it, she shakily picked up the dagger and goblet.

"Now," she said firmly, as she turned back to Travis, "lift up your arm."

Unable to resist, Travis did so, and with a violent *slash* that should have been impossible for someone of her frailty she cut at the palm of his left hand.

Blood sprayed from the wound and the old woman rushed to gather it up in the goblet, making aberrant gluttonous sounds in her throat, like a drooling beast in expectation of a feed. Once the chalice was full to the brim and overflowing, she pulled away from Travis and lapped at it hungrily, taking hideous gulps.

Her face and clothing now smeared in his blood, she returned to the table, opened the small chest and poured the goblet's remainder on to the objects within. Once the final drop had been poured, she closed the casket once more.

She clicked her tongue, to which her snarling dog responded immediately. "Go on," she called with a sickly sweetness, "help yourself now." Obediently, the dog moved forward, and began to lick at the drops of blood still pouring from Travis's wound.

After a minute or so she called the dog to heel, and picked up the white handkerchief. "That's enough now, boy; he's going to need his stamina." She moved back to Travis and shakily bound his wound with the handkerchief.

"You know," began the ancient woman, in a mock-conspiratorial tone, "Dominic wishes to invoke the Ceremony of Resurrection - so that he and his grubby little band of musicians can *live again*."

Lucretia's face contorted, as if in disgust at the prospect. "What *insolence* he had - taking my family name for himself, just because he was briefly my acolyte. I ask you; what choice did I have but to arrange for all their deaths?"

Travis said nothing in return. How could he; trapped as he was within a body he no longer controlled.

"As you know, he has reached out to you, to help him fulfil his wishes. But what Dominic *doesn't* realise is that in doing so, he will return the Ravenstone amulet from the Aetheric World - something *I greatly wish to happen*. Once his body is made whole again, so shall the amulet become solid also - and it will *feast* on his resurrected flesh the instant he returns."

Lucretia Ravenstone continued, seemingly enjoying the revelation of her deception. "And then it is a simple matter of *you* returning the pendant to *me*, so that it can take its rightful place back in these walls."

Looking Travis in the eyes once more, she indicated to the box on the table, and gave it a little tap. "Now; pick this up, and run along. There are certain things in there that shall be needed for the ceremony. You'll *know* what to do with them when the time comes."

Without saying a word, Travis picked up the blood-soaked casket and began the lengthy journey home.

In this universe, there has to be polar opposites. North to south, Yin to yang, black to white, matter to anti-matter, truth to untruth, good to evil. Call them whatever you will.

Within this tale, it would be fair to say Mary Mulcahy was the polar opposite to Lucretia Ravenstone - and as a result it would fall to her to redress the balance of the pendulum swinging very much in Lucretia's favour.

During the night Travis had received instructions to travel to Chichester, Mary had suffered unsettling dreams; images of all Travis had talked about, interwoven with her own memories of the band and the days when everything seemed to turn sour.

She tried to contact him the following day, but got no response on the number he'd left her.

Part of her wanted to leave things be; after all, she had enough on her own plate as it was, what with trying to look after two dozen demanding moggies - but try as she might she couldn't get the visions from her bad night's sleep out of her head. In fact, it seemed to make things worse; whereas dreams usually fade as a day progresses, they seemed to be worsening and becoming more vivid as the day wore on.

The dreams in the night that followed were the worst for her.

It seemed as though she were looking through Travis's *own* eyes, but trapped and immobile as he caught a train and a cab, then staggered to the doorway of a dilapidated old mansion in the sticks. There was an old *witch* waiting for him - there was no other word she could conjure in her mind, for the ancient hag gave off such a feeling of sickly evil to Mary - and she looked-on as the bizarre ritual with the knife and the blood and the box played out, and felt the rough tongue of the woman's vicious-looking hound as it lapped blood from

Travis's hand.

She heard the words the old woman had spoken; poisonous, boastful words about her family link to that damn amulet - and then watched as Travis collected the box on the woman's command and begin to walk back the way he had come. And she *knew* her, she suddenly realised, that old witch; from back in the day. She'd seen her bfore; she *knew* it.

Mary woke with a gasping start at this point, looking down to see her bedclothes soaked in sweat. She *had* to go and help Travis - and knew exactly where to go.

Travis entered the six-digit code to the Astoria Theatre's back entrance, and waited for the audible beep that indicated the alarm system had been turned off. In regards to how he knew this code, one can only assume it was just part of the information he had received from the malevolent forces that were now firmly in control of his mind.

He propped the back door open with a chair he found close to the exit, and began carrying to the stage area the supplies he had purchased earlier in the day.

Once there, he laid the supplies out and began his work. After levering open a tin of white paint, he began painting a pentagram symbol on to the floor of the stage.

With the accuracy of the angles and the perfection of the painted circle in which he enclosed it, an onlooker would think he had used measuring tools to achieve the design - but as I say, other forces were in control of Travis that evening.

Once the symbol was complete, he placed large black candles at the five points of the upturned pentagram star, before lighting each one.

He then placed the chest Lucretia Ravenstone had given him at the lowest of the five points, and opened its blood-stained lid. He removed the blood-clotted handkerchief from his wounded hand and squeezed the cut hard, forcing the knitting flesh open to release a fresh stream of blood on to the five items inside. He then proceeded to drain drips of blood on to each of the five black candles, before returning to the chest. Reaching inside, he removed the five items he had fetched from the manor house outside Chichester, and placed these on the tips of the pentangle, beside the candles.

Once this final act was complete, he seated himself within the centre of the pentagram.

His contribution to the ritual preparations done, all he had to do now was wait.

Mary Mulcahy cursed at how utterly *rubbish* her car was, and how selfishly inconvenient other drivers were. After a tortuous battle to actually get the thing started, she'd only realised that both headlights had failed after she'd had numerous minor prangs and scrapes with all the unseen parked cars and vans that were annoyingly stationed between her home and the Astoria Theatre.

It was nothing short of a miracle that she didn't get pulled over by a lurking police car - then again, it was nearly 3 a.m., and if you're going to cause carnage that was probably the best time to do it. No doubt the city's CCTV recordings would be mulled over during the coming days, when a host of insurance claims by irate drivers were phoned in.

Once she'd arrived, Mary parked close by. All seemed undisturbed at the front of the theatre, and she took a moment to wonder if this situation was completely bonkers - just some mad idea that had been somehow triggered by talking with the desperate-looking lad who'd turned up at her door not even two days earlier.

No, she told herself. Those dreams were too real - and they had the same nauseating resonance she remembered from the last days of her time in the band. *This is real, all right.*

She looked through the front windows of the theatre - through to the box office and the waiting area - but there was no sign of light.

She remembered the rear exit, however, having used it when she'd visited the theatre once or twice over the years - it was down the side alley to the right of the building.

Walking round, she noticed the alley was pitch black - and naturally she hadn't thought to fetch a torch. Mustering courage, she strode into the darkness, hoping there'd be nothing nastier than a dollop of dog muck waiting for her in the darkness.

She was in luck, and eventually noticed a sliver of light from where she vaguely recalled the exit to be; the door had been left open.

Nothing for it then, but to walk right in.

The shock of what Mary 'walked right in on' caused her heart to skip a beat and her stomach to tie itself up in knots.

During the time it had taken her to (badly) drive to the Astoria, Travis had been fulfilling the tasks he had been assigned by his malevolent masters. Once all was complete and he had placed himself at the centre of the pentangle, he watched blank-eyed as a yellowish vapour began to thicken from each of the five corners of the upended star.

But the vapours didn't come from the candles positioned there - instead, they rose from the scraps of gristle and flesh Lucretia Ravenstone had retrieved from each body of the bandmembers shortly after their deaths years earlier - the five items Travis had fetched from the manor house in the wooden casket.

From Dominic's remains, Lucretia had taken a clump of the hair-encrusted meat of his burnt scalp after the fire at the Astoria. Stumpy Moncreiff meanwhile had, as you may recall, been skinned alive, and so a ragged strip of his torn, shrivelled flesh and skin had been lain on the *second* point of the pentangle. A coil of Chipper Harris's shrunken stomach remains sat on the third point like some hideously deformed snake, while the blackened stump of one of Nobby Greenhalf's chewed hands rested on the fourth point. Finally, we come to Harry Phipps - half of his shattered skull sat on the fifth angle, with the withered remains of facial muscles, skin and hair still partially attached to much of it.

Rather than disperse outwardly, the vapours from these ghoulish remains continued to rise upward, until the shapes of five semi-translucent human figures could be determined, each bathed in a nauseating amber glow. Eventually, the resurrected Dominic Ravenstone was whole-enough to be able to smile darkly and look on each of his four bandmembers in turn. They had been returned.

But they were yet to be *free*. To be unbound from the five

points of the pentangle to which each had been summoned, he would need the amulet to feed off Travis's life-force.

Mary ran at the stage, knowing only that she had to somehow drag the mindless Travis from the centre of the circle and away from this evil. The rising yellow mists were painful to look at, and they emitted a foul pungency that made it hard to breathe.

Her arrival had not gone unobserved, however, and in a lightning-fast response to her approach Dominic cast a protection spell about the ring, knocking her backwards and propelling her through the air.

"It's good to see you after all these years, Mary," Dominic mocked as he looked over at her splayed body on the floor in front of the stage. "But don't be in such a hurry; we shall renew our relationship soon enough."

Dominic began to laugh and turned his attention to the insentient Travis sitting in the centre of the pentangle - the boy was playing his part well. Muttering the first of the 'completion' incantations, Dominic brought him out of his unconsciousness.

As Travis began to awaken, he *lived* the dream vision he had experienced whilst listening to the album days earlier in his flat. He felt the songs playing once more, overlaying and cascading with chants and conjurations that made him rise to his feet and come toward the semi-material ghost of Dominic Ravenstone.

The source of the sickly yellow light - the amulet - revealed itself to Travis, and he felt powerless as it lured him forward, *begging* him, *commanding* him to reach out and grasp it for himself.

"*That's it*, boy," coaxed Dominic's thunderously commanding voice, "... yeees, take it. All earthly pleasures can be yours. Success, power ... *whatever* your desires. Just offer yourself without reserve and take the amulet in your hand."

In Travis's mind *another* voice intermingled with that of Dominic's; Lucretia Ravenstone's ancient rasp gave Travis her *own* instructions, forcing him to a halt. "Just *leave it*, you fool! Let him materialise whole and the amulet will *eat his soul*! *Then* you can bring it to me!"

A *third* voice came then, so much weaker than the others, but just as determined - and when it spoke it felt like white air blowing against two battling storms. "Step out of the circle, Travis! You *have* to step out of the circle!"

Dominic bellowed a victorious laugh as he saw his flesh had finally been made whole, but his smile of cruel satisfaction turned to one of rage as he saw Travis falter. He thrust images of ambition and power into the young man's mind, to counter the effects of whatever was giving the boy the strength to resist. "Just reach out and *take it* ... it can all be yoursss!"

Travis wilted, and staggered back wailing. His mind could take no more. As he retreated, Dominic felt the power of the amulet *surging, demanding*; it wanted the boy's soul *now*.

No. It wanted *his*.

Dominic screamed as an arc of twisting yellow flame thrust forward from the pendant and passed around the five points of the pentagram. His bandmembers called out in their confusion as they felt the amulet draining their resurrected souls, *gorging* itself on their revitalised forms.

"Wh-what ... what *deception* is this?" cried Dominic, as

he felt his spirit's aether begin to fade from the solid form it had all-too-fleetingly taken.

He looked on the collapsed Travis in his desperation, but could see or feel nothing from him. He looked out at Mary, who was slowly regaining her footing, but saw only white light. No; this dark duplicity came from elsewhere else. He screamed again as the shrieking laugh of Lucretia Ravenstone filled his mind, and all became clear to him as he faded away.

Silence filled the theatre, and the foul, yellow vapours began to dissipate.

Slowly rising to her feet, Mary called out to Travis. There was no response, so she headed toward him. "Are you alright there, Travis? Come on, it's okay now - let's get you home." Mumbling comments under her breath about needing a chiropractor to sort her back out after that fall, she painfully walked the side stairs on to the stage - and stopped to study the remains of the black ceremony once she was on the boards.

"Well, the janitor's going to be in for a shock when he sees all *this* shite," she sighed to herself. "But let's get you sorted out in the meanti-."

The moment Mary stepped inside the circle, a voice that sounded like the cawing of a thousand starving ravens suddenly shrieked within her mind. "I sense a *white witch*," Lucretia Ravenstone screamed at her.

Mary gasped and fell on her knees as the pain of the voice drilled deep into her skull. She felt Lucretia scouring her mind for information and gasped once more as an all-but-forgotten memory was nonchalantly plucked out of her thoughts and laid in front of her.

It was a memory from Mary's final days with the band, when she was leaving a party they had all attended. Standing on the steps of the venue, she lit a cigarette and watched a huge white car roll up in front of the party. Dominic was heading down the steps, but instead of noticing her he carried on toward the car as if spellbound by it. She noticed how the blackened rear windows were slightly lowered as Dominic approached; words were silently exchanged and the door opened to let him slip inside. She'd caught a glimpse of the woman through the window, and remembered shivering at the sight of the emaciated old woman seated inside.

"Lucretia," Mary managed to fearfully say as the memory passed.

"Mary," came the ice-cold response in her mind. Mary felt the oppressiveness of Lucretia's power lighten slightly, and saw some reaction in Travis as it was focussed on him instead. The voice in her mind continued, however.

"Boy; you have done *well*. The amulet has been freed and you can return it to me."

The amulet. Mary's mind raced; memories of Dominic wearing that hideous thing and all that Travis had told her about it when he came to see her. *Lucretia wants it so badly - but wouldn't it have disappeared when Dominic did?* No - there it was! On the point of the pentangle where he'd risen.

Mary made a lunge for the amulet, but found her battered body and Lucretia's presence in her mind made her movements feel like she was wading in treacle.

And then there was the problem of Travis now reaching out for her, his hands grasping for her throat.

That hideous voice in her mind again. "You shouldn't

have *interfered*, Mary," it said, now with an abhorrent cackle. "Still, while you're here ..."

Mary gagged and choked as Travis's hands gained purchase around her neck. Ignoring the pain, and her head swimming, she forced herself on - until the amulet was only one further stretch away.

But Mary could reach no further, and felt a tide of white light wash over her. Instead of trying to fight and resist any longer she felt herself relax - her hands instinctively reaching for the crucifix about her neck.

All at once she felt Lucretia's violation wither back from her mind like burning weeds and Travis's clenched hands fall away.

She gasped as air began to return to her pain-wracked lungs and opened streaming eyes to see life and consciousness return to Travis's *own* eyes.

Suddenly, as if knowing exactly what they needed to do, he reached out for the amulet and brought it in front of Mary. It still emitted its sickly yellow aura but it seemed to be so much weaker now.

Mary pulled at her necklace, until the crucifix broke free. Clasping his hands in her own, they brought it down on the amulet like a hammer on an anvil.

Blood ran from their ears and eyes as Lucretia's shriek of frustration rang through their minds. They huddled together in fear as a sudden wind blew through the theatre, while flames began to spontaneously ignite throughout the building.

And unbeknownst to Travis and Mary at that moment, the same was simultaneously happening to the decrepit old manor house near Chichester.

Travis managed to get Mary to her feet, and bundled her off the stage in the direction of the exit. The swirling winds soon made the fires a raging furnace, and neither looked back as wailing screams followed them along the passages.

They had to avoid flames and falling debris, but managed to make it out alive.

Travis carried Mary down the alley beside the theatre, and finally got her to her car. They turned around one last time to see the whole of the Astoria going up in flames, before driving off into the night.

The fire services came and dealt with the fire, while the police arrived to begin their preliminary investigations. All agreed it was doubtful the Astoria would be rebuilt again - two gutting fires occurring in the same way within a period of twenty years or so meant there must be some kind of design flaw to the building; a ventilation issue, perhaps. Besides that, the insurance would be astronomical.

After half a day of dousing, dampening and checking the overall structure was safe to enter, the fire crew began to wind up their work. The eldest of the team was Big Bill Patterson, and his final task that day was to give the last of the smoking embers in the stage area a final soaking with the hose to ensure nothing could reignite.

Once he'd almost finished, Bill noticed something with a metallic glint among the ash and debris. With a charred stick he scraped away some of the debris at his feet to find two ... what ... pendants? Pieces of jewellery? Slyly glancing around in case any the police were watching, he reached down to pick them both up.

One was a small cross, that had been melted and warped almost beyond recognition in the heat. But the other ... now *that* was more interesting. *A star-shaped medallion*, that was the best way he could describe it. Strangely enough it had remained completely unscathed, despite the heat; it just needed a bit of a buff with a cloth, and it'd be good as new. *What was that shape called again?*, Bill mused to himself. Not a pentagon ... ahh, *a pentangle*, that was it. He'd seen the same symbol on some of his daughter's tattoos - and God knows she had enough of them, plastered all over her arms and neck. He frowned and shook his head at the thought.

The ageing fireman took a final look at the twisted crucifix and tossed it back amongst the charred timbers. "Melted slag - no use to anybody, that," he mumbled, and didn't give it another thought.

The pentangle amulet was worth another look though, and he liked how it gave off an unearthly glow, and seemed to *shimmer* in the light.

"She'd like this as a present, would Peggy," he mumbled to himself, wiping some of its surface clean with his gloved fingers. "Reckon I'll take it down to the music shop and give it to her in the morning, once my shift's finished." Glancing around a final time to check for his workmates and the police, he quietly slipped it into an overall pocket and headed back to the fire engine.

THE END

THE WITCH'S SKULL

My name is Martin Jeddoe, and as this is the last night my mortal soul shall remain upon the Good Lord's Earth, I hereby write my testament of all that has transpired since my return from war.

It is the year sixteen hundred and forty-six, and I have been a Captain of Oliver Cromwell's New Model Army. I had been away for seven months in our nation's bloody Civil War before the supernatural events that lead to my imprisonment within these walls. I do not use the word supernatural lightly, for although it is a Godless word I can think of none more suitable.

The war has taken some toll on me, and my right arm is now injured as a consequence of battle with the infernal Royalists. My platoon's apothecarie told me my sword-fighting days were over, and I have in recent weeks been reduced to issuing commands instead of throwing myself into combat, as has always been my preference. The wound caused me a grave sickness and maladie over the winter, and in truth my soldiers said I should have returned some months ago, were not the press of battle so severe that all good Parliamentarian men were needed these past two seasons.

Yet nothing would prevent me from returning home when duty allowed, and to my new wife, sweet Elisabeth, and so it was that on the first day of March I did return to my homestead.

As I passed the brook that runs strongly past the wheatfields on my village's outskirts, I was filled with joy as I saw Hoefolk's thatched roofs and church spire for the first time since last summer.

Hoefolk was curiously quiet as I rode into the village on that fateful morning - one would normally be met by the bustle of market traders readying their stalls, the peel of bells for church service and the sound of livestock being herded toward the village square for sale.

On this morning, however, all house doors and shutters were closed, and a stray wandering goose was the only sign I could see of life.

There had been a bonfire, I noticed, for I saw the charred remains of a blackened patch of cobbles in the middle of the village square. Smoke still rose from the last of the embers, which led me to surmise the fire had only been burning the day or evening before, and there were many charred timbers and burnt hay bales scattered about the square; leftovers, no doubt, from the building of the fire. I deduced that whatever revelry had taken place had been the reason for the village's empty streets this following morning, but at the time thought little of it - so keen was I to get home.

I soon arrived at the gate of our cottage, knowing my arrival without announcement would make my reunion with Elisabeth all the merrier.

Tying Ironsides (my horse) to a post I dismounted and made speed through our home's open door, calling my dear wife Elisabeth's name aloud.

But I stopped in horror at what I found inside.

The house had been ransacked - every piece of furniture had been either upended, shredded or broken into pieces. And it was the same wherever I went - bags of food in the pantry had been torn open and were a haven for mice, rugs and drapes had been torn and shredded and windows broken. Drawers in our cupboards had been emptied - as if searched - and left on the floor. Finally, I ran upstairs - my heart pounding at what I might discover - and gasped as I found *one word* had been daubed in black pitch across the wall above our bed.

Witch.

I called Elisabeth's name aloud, though I knew at that point our cottage was deserted. I opened the window to the rear of the building and called out to the pretty garden of roses that Elisabeth loved to tend - but again, she was nowhere to be seen, and no answer could be heard.

In my frustration, I ran downstairs and beat on the door of our neighbour and good friend, Bethany Wells - surely she would have word of what had happened in my absence.

I briefly saw two red pinpricks of light in the darkness, beyond a gap in her window shutters. It was a curious thing to behold in the light of day - almost like the eyes of a fox or cat at night when a lantern is shone on them - and then they were gone.

But then I heard the noise of what sounded like someone clumsily knocking over a chair - and knew in an instant my neighbour was hiding herself from my view.

In my desperate fury, I kicked at her door until it gave way - and she gave out a scream as I stormed into her home. As I had thought, she had been hiding herself away in darkness behind closed shutters and I pushed one open that I might see her more clearly.

I was shocked at what I beheld when the sun's rays were cast on her; Bethany carried wounds and dark bruising all about her face and body, and seemed fey and agitated in her manner. She winced when I tried to reach out to her, and quickly slid back into the shadows, where she seemed to find some modicum of peace.

"Bethany," I called to her across the room, "I can see there's much that has transpired while I have been absent, of which you must tell me, and I'm truly sorry for the desperate condition you find me in - but you *must* tell me what has happened to my Elisabeth."

At this she began to wail and cry uncontrollably, and I couldn't make hide nor hair of the garbled words she was trying to tell me, despite my efforts of consolation. But eventually she calmed, and I daresay I went white in disbelief at the story she had to tell …

Bethany told me that two weeks prior to my return, none other than Matthew Hopkins - the *Witchfinder General* - and his entourage had made their way to Hoefolk.

As any reader of this testament will surely know, Hopkins has spent years travelling through the land in his alleged quest to root out witches, and uses methods of persuasion on the accused that most would consider barbaric. Indeed, as it was Hopkins that placed me in the gaol in which I now languish, and have fell foul of the tools of his interrogation, I can acknowledge this latter fact to be true.

But I have diverted from my recollections, and shall now

return to them ...

Bethany told me that upon arrival in Hoefolk, Hopkins declared to all within the village that he had heard news of acts of witchcraft and Godless devilry being perpetrated within the region, and that he had come to *enact a purgery*. Where the Witchfinder General had heard such news remained a mystery, she told me, as it was only after his arrival that *strange, uncanny acts* were known to have occurred.

I asked her what she meant by this, to which she responded by returning to the mood of hysteria in which I first found her. It ails me to write it now, but I felt it such a matter of importance I was somewhat forceful with her.

In time, her mood became more tranquil and she began to laugh - but it was an *hysterical* laugh; the kind you will hear from the crazed and the deranged, and I will admit it caused me great disturbance. *Look about the village, Captain*, was all she would say, *and then you'll see what Old Bethany means.*

It was a struggle for her to say anything of *reason* thereafter, and I fear recent events have sent her into madness. I pressed her on what Hopkins and his men had done and most importantly what had happened to Elisabeth, which only brought the onset of more hysteria. But I would not be ignored and forced these final, terrible words from her - words that brought a chill to my heart and broke it ...

She's dead! Don't you understand? Burned alive for witchery like all those others! And then that sickening laughter returned.

My head reeling from these words, I ran back to the heart

of the village, falling to the ground in disbelief in the centre of the charred cobble stones where the bonfire had taken place. Surely no such act of cruelty and madness could have happened in this enlightened age? I ran my hands and fingers over the stones, trying to find some shred of evidence amongst the burnt straw and ash to prove or disprove what Bethany Wells had said.

With a gasp, I soon found sickening evidence to give truth to her words.

Human bones.

And Elisabeth's wedding ring.

I cried then, I am not ashamed to say. Long and hard amidst the smoking ruins of that damned fire. I would never wish such anguish on any man nor woman.

I cannot tell you how long I lay there, but know only that after a time I became aware of voices in my mind. They were quiet at first, but then became louder - I think it took some time for me to hear them in my anguish, so distracted was I. But when I did hear them, they chilled my heart - for it was *laughter* once more that I could hear, from many voices; the kind of giddy laughter you would hear from children, but *deeper* in tone, as with the voices of a man and woman.

This incensed me, and I rose in anger to my feet; how dare *anyone* laugh at another in such suffrage or at the fate of their spouse! I looked around to assail those persons who thought it humourous to have such cruel mirth, but there was no-one to see.

I felt then that I needed the comfort of our Lord, and though numbed by the revelations thus far I made my way to our village's church.

When I arrived I went straight to Father Wyatt, a good priest I have known most of my life, who I could see was in the process of preparation for the morning's service. A few men and women were waiting on their pews for the service to commence, but I gave them little heed.

Upon seeing me, Father Wyatt broke from his work, bade me welcome and we talked.

"My son," he said soothingly, "Elisabeth's soul is now at peace - find solace in that."

"S-so it's true, then," I weakly replied, "my dear Elisabeth was ... was burned as a witch. But why did no-one try and *stop* that fiend Hopkins? Our village has enough strong men to deal with his rogues!"

At this, Father Wyatt looked confused, and I recoiled from the words that followed.

"But my son, why should anyone feel need to intervene? Our Witchfinder General has done God's work these past days, and our village is now *cleansed*. It is only a shame you were tardy in your travels, for had you arrived only yesterday you could have witnessed the glorious, purifying fires as they took Elisabeth's corrupted flesh from this Earth."

One day. I had arrived just one day too late to save her.

"But why would he select Elisabeth?" I wailed, clinging to his robes. "She was so pure of heart - you know this yourself, Father."

"Alas, but Satan has so many ways to deceive," he replied. "The Witchfinder General knew evil lies best in the heart of *a woman alone*, for she is wanton, and deceitful - they will take the newborn and devour them, and indulge in many other wicked acts of devilry. He gathered all the women without husbands and put them to trial these past days, and he proved it to be so."

He rubbed a hand over my head, as if petting a child, before continuing. "Even I at first doubted that the Devil's work could reside within your Elisabeth, but thorough methods used proved it correct. He put six women to trial - and five were proven guilty. And the screams, my son, *the screams* - such melodies. By the end of their torture, it was only Elisabeth who would not confess - more proof toward her *guilt*, Hopkins advised."

Truly I could not believe that such words were coming from a man of God - but he continued; "Your neighbour, Bethany Wells, was also put to trial, but passed the tests and was freed. Hopkins' decreed *the Lord* worked within her, not Satan, for she withstood all tortures and blissfully laughed throughout her trials."

I heard *more* laughter then; the childish kind I had heard before, and looked about the church. It was coming from the parishioners; Tom Burbidge and his wife Emily; Jack Harris the carpenter, and his two daughters; John Buchan and his son James.

And I shuddered in revulsion at their appearances, for all had been marked with hideously bulbous poxes and pustules, as if carrying the plague - yet seemed not to notice. I grasped Tom Burbidge by the lapels of his coat, desperately trying to shake some sense out of him, but he merely laughed and spat at me from scabrous lips in response, the vileness of his breath so toxic I was almost overpowered by its rank stench.

More villagers arrived, and more began to laugh and screech upon sight of me. People I had called friends all my life - my head rang at the insanity of it all.

"I must commence the service," Father Wyatt said, and he returned to his pulpit.

I sat for a while on the front aisle in my malaise, wanting to pray for Elisabeth's soul - but the words from our priest were not as I knew our services to be, and I felt sickened by what sounded to be more like a dirge of chants than hymns from the assembled.

Father Wyatt had taken on a different countenance upon the pulpit, I quickly observed - his words were full of anger and glory and triumph, and ominously dark in tone, which the congregation appeared to revel in.

And then the foulest act of all came, when two of the assembled came to the pulpit, carrying a writhing sack. Father Wyatt reached into it and dragged out a bleating lamb, before cruelly cutting its throat and thrusting the bleeding wound to his mouth.

"Enough!" I shouted, drawing my sword and ready then to strike even Father Wyatt down. "What insane *Godlessness* is this?"

To which I was met with more wicked mirth. Roaring, heartless laughter from all the congregation. I looked back at the man that had once been my old friend Father Wyatt, and my heart was crushed when I saw he was laughing loudest of all, his lips peeled back in his blood-soiled face to reveal gnashing teeth and his eyes so bulging he looked to be screaming rather than laughing.

"This - this place is *cursed*!" I shouted in stupefied response. Only *the Devil* resides here now!"

The laughter continued as I staggered out of the church

and back toward the town.

As I passed the square once more, I saw that the village had come to life during my time at the church - men, women and children were now wandering the streets, all seemingly afflicted by the same poxes and madness I'd seen in the church. I saw children clawing viciously at their own faces, while their own parents stood by and laughed. I saw men laughing and throwing themselves from the top of their homes to break their own necks or bury their heads into water troughs so they might drown themselves, while women with lit torches oiled their own clothing and set themselves aflame. I saw debauchery and violence everywhere; I had been sickened by things I had witnessed when at war, yet nothing compared to this. Was there *no* sanity left in this village?

It was clear to me Hopkins and his men had left the village, as after an hour of searching they could not be found. I decided then to take to the road again, to the villages north of Hoefolk - as my journey up from the south had been peaceful and eventful. I returned to my cottage and untethered Ironsides, and we started our journey - but not before I heard more goading laughter resume from Old Bethany's home.

A wicked thought passed over me in that moment; one in which I would enter her home once more and run her through with my sword. But I had no proof she was to blame for anything that had happened, and I will admit there was still some part of my heart hoping that Elisabeth was still alive - that the bones I had seen amongst the ashes were not hers.

I decreed I would get all my answers from Matthew

Hopkins himself, and set off.

North of Hoefolk is the hamlet of Jarvale, and I am sad to say I found it much as I had found my home village. The church was aflame, and many of the villagers were in a ring within the market square, laughing and dancing dementedly as an unfortunate pair of souls were being burned at the stake.

I espied two elderly men dressed in black, who appeared to be overseeing proceedings; but Hopkins was not one of them. I had seen him once from afar, whilst on one of my military campaigns, and knew him to be only a young man, despite his fearsome reputation. I deduced a tiny hamlet like Jarvale didn't warrant his personal attention, and that he had left this place to his lackeys.

There was nothing I could do for those poor, burning unfortunates, so I passed through quickly lest I attract attention myself, and shuddered at how rapidly this madness had afflicted the folk of Jarvale. If Hopkins and his men had only left Hoefolk yesterday, then they must have only stayed in Jarvale for a matter of hours - so they must surely be only a mile or two ahead of me.

My suspicion proved correct, for as my horse cantered along the winding lanes that lead from Jarvale to the nearby town of Wheatton I caught sight of a band of men and horses some two hundred yards distant.

I dismounted and pulled Ironsides into the shade beneath an oak tree on the edge of a row of barley and corn fields, and watched as they slowly made their way over the final hill towards the outskirts of the next town. They were too far away for me to see clearly, but I counted at least a dozen men before they past over the crest of the hill and disappeared from sight.

Thinking of the Witchfinder's men back in Jarvale, I became conscious of being so visible and alone in daylight, and realised it would be safer to approach the next town by night. I also realised I hadn't eaten, so pulled Ironsides further into the shade and away from the lane, tethered her to the oak and slipped back to Jarvale for supplies.

With the hamlet in such uproar, no-one noticed as I raided an abandoned house on the edge of the village, and returned with some cheese, bread and wine for myself and a couple of apples for Ironsides some two hours after I'd left.

Evening wasn't far off at that point, and I sat concealed beneath that hefty old oak. In my grief and weariness I am ashamed to say I fell asleep beneath that tree, as the sun began to set over the low, rolling hills to the west of the fields nearby.

I woke with a start, though I had no knowledge as to what time it might be; the day had gone, and only the last of the sun's rays could be seen over the hills in the distance. An hour or more could have passed, for all I knew.

Beneath the light of the rising moon, I could make out the silhouette of Ironsides as he contentedly nibbled away at barley chaff on the nearby field, and the remains of the apples I had fetched.

It was then that I saw my beautiful Elisabeth standing in the field in front of me.

It could be no other; dressed in the white dress she had worn on our wedding day and looking as beautiful and radiant as the first day I had met her. She seemed to *glide* across the land as she came toward me, and I lurched forward from my reclined posture against the tree in my shock and wonder so that I might welcome her.

"C-can it be?" I recall myself calling out. "Elisabeth - is it truly you? I heard such ill news - I-I feared you we-."

She hushed me with gentle words. "Be calmed, my love," she whispered. "All will be well - but I am not as once I was."

She looked down then, and following the path of her eyes I realised the true meaning of her words. As I strode forward to embrace her I saw the distant moon and the stubbled chaff of the field through her dress - through *her* - and I realised what she was - a mere apparition; a phantom.

"No," I sobbed then, shaking my head in realisation. "No, Elisabeth - it cannot be. It *can't*."

"It *is*," she replied, "and I am. But *fear not*, my brave, noble husband - for all is not yet lost. You must go to Hopkins - he is not all he seems. He can *return me* to the mortal world; he has the ability to do so."

"*Return* you?" I replied in my confusion. "My dearest - I do not understand."

"He has my *skull*," she said then. Four words which made me shiver in horror and shake in anger.

She continued. "The Witchfinder General is the grandest of deceivers; he conceals all that he is by making play of punishing innocents. As I have been *unmade*, so too can I be *made whole* once more."

"Then he is a witch *himself*?" I gasped then.

"Perhaps much more," the spirit of Elisabeth replied. "People believe Hopkins seeks out witchcraft, but in truth he brings it with him; wherever he journeys he leaves a trail of madness, evil and plague in his wake - as I am sure you have discovered."

"Damnation sweeps our village," I answered. "All is lost. Father Wyatt was insane, as was Old Bethany - she, I believe, may be part of the cause; her eyes were like the fires of hell and she had an insidious manner about her."

"Not so," my Elisabeth replied. "They are both pawns in the Witchfinder's game. Bethany I believe was left alive for you to find, so she might goad you on your return."

"Then I must stop him, somehow," I replied fervently, "or this evil will spread like a canker. I will gather my troops and we'll run Hopkins and his acolytes down. I'll see him hanging from the gallows yet."

"But you cannot," she replied simply. "You are not dealing with an ordinary man, as I have said."

"But how could I get such a man - if indeed he *be* a man - to do as you have told me - to make you whole once more?"

"He will ask a question of you," she answered, "and you will know what to say when the time comes."

And with those final words she faded from my view.

We left then for Wheatton, Ironsides and I. It was only a mile or so to the town, as I have said, and on our approach I witnessed more of the Godless madness Hopkins had created; wildness and foul behaviour amongst the populace, the screams of the insane and many homes ablaze.

More innocents had, it seemed, been chosen by the raving citizens to be tried for witchcraft, as several were being dragged toward the town's pond - two more of the Witchfinder's men were already there overseeing matters, and I could see the limp forms of two drowned women being removed from the waters.

I dismounted and left Ironsides untethered; I would not leave him at the mercy of others. I then carried on alone through the town, and was met by a pair of fevered rogues who thought it wise to assault me. Despite my wound, they were no match for my sword and I put a swift end to their madness.

Ahead of me soon was the town hall, and in front of its Tudor masonry stood the man I had come to find.

The Witchfinder General had perhaps nine or ten of his lackeys with him, all of whom seemed casually preoccupied with the merciless task of 'trying witches'. A line of bound, screaming townsfolk - both men and women - were being cruelly tortured with a host of iron devices his men carried about their person.

They had horses with them, I noticed, and an entourage of servants, along with carts carrying barrels and crates of supplies; everything Hopkins needed for life on the road.

I had kept to the shadows as I approached, though this was soon proven pointless. Breaking away from his despicable work, Hopkins looked in my direction - as if his piercing eyes could easily see into the darkness - and gave salute.

"You are welcome here, Captain," he called out, "and my men shall make no hostile move toward you."

Understanding my attempt at concealment had failed, I

warily left the shadows and made my way toward the Witchfinder General and his men - who were all dressed in fine black silk, as was their master. The heads of his acolytes were shaven, I noticed, and each carried strange markings and sigils on the skin of their scalps, as I have sometimes seen on sailors and natives of other lands.

"Ah, the noble Captain Jeddoe," said Hopkins, as I approached. "And husband to Elisabeth of Hoefolk, unless I am mistaken."

"That I am, Sir," I replied coldly, "though how you know this I do not know. And I know who *you* are, Witchfinder General - though in truth Witch*maker* should be thy title, for any sane man would see that it is *you* who are responsible for the devilry that has cursed wherever you have trodden. And though it would surely please me most to run you through with my sword for payment of the wicked things I know you have accomplished, I stand here in the hope you will undo what has been done to my bride - if indeed that be within your power."

Hopkins smiled at me then as he summed me up, and offered a courteous bow in response to my riposte.

He was a young man, as I have said - or at least his outward countenance was that of a young man's; in truth, I felt there and then that if you scratched away his sublime veneer you would find something foul, ancient and decrepit beneath. He began to circle me slowly, like a wild predator circles its prey, and I shuddered as I felt an aura of sinister, undeniable power from this man as he passed around me. I felt then that even if I had tried to strike him down with my sword - and struck true at his heart - it would have come to nothing.

He gave word to his men to break from their heinous torture of the innocents, and the bound accused were led away to the town's gaol - a place I would be taken to myself, soon enough.

"You say I have done wicked things?" Hopkins replied in a gentle mocking tone. "I say I have done no wickedness, Captain; I have merely set the people free from all their suffering. For years they have endured war, famine, sickness and the austerities our King and Cromwell have bestowed upon them all; I have merely passed among them and enlightened them with my gifts. But you speak to me also of 'undoing' that which I have done to your sweet Elisabeth, so I must ask you, Sir - what would you give *in return*? What would *you* offer so she might live and breathe once more?"

At this I had no answer at first; what could I possibly offer a man like this as payment? Money? Power? He had both already, whilst I had little. My service, then? Could I work for this fiend, if he asked it of me - and again, what would he need of an injured soldier when he could summon a legion to do his bidding? I thought then back to the field, and the oak tree - my meeting with Elizabeth's spirit. She had said I would know what to say when the time came.

"I would give *anything*, Matthew Hopkins - as you must surely know."

"Indeed," he replied, turning on his heel to face me. "*Anything*. Your soul, perhaps?"

"Anything," I answered without hesitation, "anything so her own body and soul can be made whole once more."

"Very well, then," Hopkins replied, and nodded to one of

his servants. Without needing further guidance, the man strode off to one of their horses and loosened a satchel tethered to its side. After delving inside it, he returned to Hopkins with a small silken bundle.

Hopkins opened the package to reveal a white human skull, the sight of which made me tremble in my anguish. It seemed so small and frail; merely some sinister object, the likes of which I had seen many times whilst at war - but it pained me to associate such a thing with my loved one.

"Your dear Elisabeth," said Hopkins, gesturing to the skull. "Now, your hand, please."

Taking my left hand, he placed Elisabeth's skull within my palm, then bade me raise my right palm also. This he cut deeply with a knife he had about his person, then placed my right hand down on to the top of the skull, so the blood which poured from the wound trickled down on to it.

Hopkins' men formed a tight circle about us then, facing inward, their eyes seemingly transfixed on what would happen next.

For my part, all I can say is no man should have to witness that which I saw in the hours that followed.

Slowly, as the blood tickled down on to the bone, the skull began to grow sinew, and muscle. Gelatinous eyes began to form within the skull's eye sockets - eyes without lids that seemed to stare into my soul as they became whole. I saw the cavity inside the bone fill - grey brain matter growing and becoming solid, before skin and hair began to form.

Soon, I was holding the head of my Elisabeth.

The vile process continued. The spine began to grow from the back of the skull, along with veins and muscles to form the neck. Soon the weight of the newly forming body became considerable and I was forced to lie it - I cannot call it *her* - on the ground, but Hopkins forebode me to release my bloodied palm from the top of Elizabeth's head lest the spell be unbroken, and I was forced to kneel beside the transforming torso.

As the hours passed, I watched the rest of the body form. I saw the recreation of Elizabeth's heart and was shocked by its first violent beat, before the thumping organ was encased by muscle and bone. I saw her growing body convulse as it took in a first lungful of air. I saw the limbs grow, inch by inch; bone, sinew, veins and finally skin.

Finally, as dawn began to break, my Elisabeth slowly rose and stood, whole and complete once more.

For a brief moment, I will admit all malice toward Hopkins ceased within me when I saw her anew and beautiful in front of me; all that mattered was Elisabeth was whole again, and he had made it so.

I wrapped my cloak about her and muttered words of silent prayer in my wonder.

"You're *whole* again, my love," I said to her, tears streaming down my face, "body and soul."

Then came the revelation that broke my heart a final time. Without prompt or calling, Elisabeth looked beyond me as if I truly did not exist - and walked directly toward the Witchfinder General.

She bowed her head to him, and he embraced her in return.

"My witch has returned," Hopkins smiled, "and you have done well."

I remember I shouted words of outrage and despair, but even as I spoke them I knew they were without hope. Within moments, the Witchfinder's men had grabbed at me, and began dragging me away to the town sheriff's gaol - in which I have languished these past three days.

And that was the last I saw of Matthew Hopkins and my Elisabeth.

My witch.

I have been informed by my gloating gaolers that I shall be burned at the stake at dawn. The official charge is to be 'for conspiring with witches'.

I care not.

I shall endure all that Elisabeth did endure, whether she be witch or otherwise.

And these pages that I write I suppose shall be confiscated and thrown on the fire also.

But I have written my last testament these past few hours, as that is all I can do, and I hereby commit my body to my Lord. I can only hope he will see fit to wrestle my soul from the Witchfinder General.

THE END

I AM A GHOST

I am a ghost. I am *the* ghost of 213 Peverill Road. I inhabited this house when I was alive, and I continue to do so now.

I have a tendency to float, high in the corners of the upstairs rooms, almost in touch with the ceiling.

I did not choose to remain in this house, nor this world. And yet I do; floating, drifting, continuing.

I have seen my spectral self in the tall, decorative mirrors that adorn many of the walls of this house; I suppose they are too heavy to remove and, I daresay, perceived as too extravagant to discard.

I float, as I have said, though my appearance is not what it once was when I was alive, nor even what one might determine to be what a ghost should look like. I am not a wailing spook with a white sheet over it, or a pale, chain-rattling gothic vision of my former self.

Instead, those mirrors throw back at me a misty *smudge* of cloudiness; a shifting, changing vapour-shape. *White steam*, I call myself. There are times, when I choose to move, that I resemble some hideous, nebulous *creature* clinging to the ceiling. And when my wispy form is at rest, I resemble a throbbing, pulsating *thing* that looks as if it will engulf you.

I found myself hideous for many years.

With such an appearance you can perhaps understand how, over the years, I have weakened people's hearts and induced screams so shrill they could surely break the glass within the frames of those long, tall mirrors.

It took me a long time to accept what I had become. For though repulsive is my appearance, malevolence is *not* my nature - and to not be a reflection of myself was always my greatest regret. For whatever reason that I am forced to remain within these walls, all I will ever do is *observe* - and never harm. I do not think myself *capable* of hurting, even if it was my desire to do so.

It is easy to divide people into two categories in reference to whether or not I am observed. Amongst the living there are, I suppose, the seers and the non-seers ... the *aware-of-me's* and the *unawares*, and I have found it a fallacy to believe that only the young or the very old are mindful of my presence. Children have seen me, and so have their parents and grandparents. So have their cats and dogs. There was even a caged parrot that seemed determined to spend all day talking to me.

I have heard people fearfully talk of me and describe me in whispers and, I'm sad to say, on some occasions they have left the house forever because of me.

I remember little of my life when I was alive. I cannot tell you what I looked like as a child, nor which of my parents I took after in terms of personality and appearance. It is only the shimmering echoes of my final days that remain.

There are no images I can recollect; only sensations. There was euphoria, at first; I was a young woman when I died, on my very own wedding day - I can recall that much.

Emmeline Digby; at least I can also remember my own name. I've always doubted anyone would remember the name Emmeline Digby, nor the person once attached to it; many families have come and gone through 213 Peverill Road, and a long time has passed since I did.

I never had chance for a family, and this saddened me greatly. There was despair, in those final days; I have recollections of my new husband losing money in a 'financial crash', days for our marriage - though I will admit that the detachments my mind has undergone means I have no real understanding of what a financial crash *is*, or was.

A man called Crabtree; that was my brief husband's name - though for some stubborn reason I insisted on retaining Digby as my surname - it's funny how dredging up these memories encourages little details like that to arise. I cannot recall my husband's Christian name, however; I suppose it's irrelevant, anyhow.

What I *do* recall is the fear and the pain; that same husband setting the house alight in some stupid, drunken act after our wedding; pride, desperation or depression, I know not. He only succeeded in burning down two upstairs rooms, in the building's annexe. And whether he knew I was in one of them, I would never find out.

The house was rebuilt where necessary, and I remained -

as some foggy, vaporous shape - left to drift from room to room, as I have mentioned.

I have no feelings of malice toward Crabtree, my briefest of husbands, and even if I had it would be of no consequence. The years pass by in this house, and through its doors new men, women and children have come and gone. Old wallpapers have been torn down to be replaced by new. Old furnitures have been moved out, and in come newer fashions.

The only constants are the walls and the rafters, the rooftiles and the creaking floorboards; the skeleton of the house. And myself, of course.

Death was a strange experience. So much pain and emotion compressed into such a mercifully short period of time, followed by an equally merciful release. It all felt like such a waste.

Coming back was even stranger. I was always taught 'you see a bright light' when you die, but when one *returns* it's quite the opposite - almost like being pulled backwards from the depths of the sea into daylight once more. It's probably different if you manage to make it to heaven, if there is one; I've often wondered if it was something I did in life that stopped me getting there?

Getting used to my new, floating, nebulous self took some getting used to, I recall. I just kept rising to the ceiling, unable to work out how to move, or how to get down from up there. I once stared at the same patch of ceiling *for a month*. And it took me *forever* to work out how to form arms and legs again, not to mention a head.

Shortly after the fire, my death and the rebuilding of the house, there was a war. I know this because of the flashes each night outside the house, along with the deafening noises, the violent shaking and the flames from other homes. I watched it all from the windows, thinking of all the other souls being lost out there. Sometimes I fancied I could even see their soul-lights drifting skyward. *Perhaps that's the trick*, I used to tell myself - *don't die indoors, or you'll be stuck down here forever.* The house lay empty for a while, until a number of wounded soldiers came to stay, along with a couple of nurses or carers of some description. I suppose the house became some kind of convalescent home during that time, due to its generous size and its proximity from anything exciting the world had to offer.

These new tenants were unable to see me, but one blinded soldier - a Corporal, I think - was able to *sense* me. He always knew there was someone with him, even when he'd thoroughly checked to make sure the others weren't hiding in the room somewhere, pulling japes.

It never bothered him, I noticed. He'd quietly call out, asking if anyone was there; I couldn't answer of course, but he'd just *know* if I was close by, and smile. He seemed grateful of the companionship. As was I.

I was always glad he couldn't see me, in a way; I myself was still getting used to my appearance and if he could have seen what I saw when I look in the mirror I fear I would have driven him half insane.

Soldiers came and went for a number of years, and I noticed

(through eavesdropping on their conversations) that the house was beginning to get a reputation for being haunted; it appeared my blind Corporal wasn't the only one to notice me.

One day the soldiers all abruptly cleared out, and a family - a mother, father and young daughter - arrived not long after. The dreadful noises and bangs and flashes outdoors had also ceased. This, I deduced, meant the war had finally ended.

The young girl picked up on me *immediately*, as did the family dog. They would both wander into the room I tended to float in (what had originally been the south-facing larger bedroom, in the annexe) and stand and stare at the corner of the room where I was trying to conceal myself. On every occasion I did my upmost not to move or cause either the child or the animal to have any fear of me.

"What's that funny *smudge* in the corner?" the daughter would ask her parents, time and time again - much to their bemusement. Eventually, the father climbed a ladder (trying to see what his daughter was going on about) and paint the walls a bright yellow to try and convince her 'the smudge' had gone.

He did this several times, but it never worked.

As she got older, the daughter made the room her study - with the desk facing toward 'my' corner, so she could squint from time to time in my direction to keep an eye on me (or suddenly look up to try and catch me out). The dog would always sit beside her - facing me, of course. Keeping my vapour-self immobile for hours on end was not an easy task, but I'd grown to love this child and her shaggy dog and it would have broken my heart to alarm her.

I was sad to see the arrival one day of cardboard boxes and packing crates; it meant only one thing - that this nice little suburban family were moving away. I remember watching their car as it left for the last time, loaded up with boxes and ephemera and the girl (who should perhaps now more accurately be described as a young woman) looking up at my window. How I wanted to extend an arm and give her a final, wispy wave of my hand - but no; she had what must have been at least ten years of hopefully happy memories in this home, and I didn't want to tarnish that with a final shock.

Next to move in were a large, some might say 'vulgar' family; all of whom were either too self-obsessed or too busy fighting with one another to notice my presence.

At least now I could wander about the house without fear of alarming anyone, and I was surprised at how much the interior had changed since the brief time I had 'physically' lived in it. The previous family had made an impressive job of renovating the house after its austere appearance during its war-time service; unfortunately this new family seemed intent on demolishing their efforts within a matter of weeks.

I can't say I was sad (or surprised) to see them go. They didn't deserve this house.

The next arrivals were another small family, and unfortunately it transpired I was *fully visible* to their young son. My heart bled as I heard his terrified screams to his mother; explaining how he could see this 'giant floating monster' living in the spare room.

I traumatised that poor child so much. If I could have *left* this house for his sake then I would, but I'm bound to its walls. If I could have changed my appearance for the sake of his sanity, then I'd have done so in an instant.

They didn't stay long, I'm sad to say, and after they left the house went unoccupied and neglected for quite some time.

Fashion (and attitudes) certainly seemed to change in the lengthy period the house was left empty. The next arrivals I could only describe as some form of 'long-haired commune', as there were *so many* of them. At least a dozen adult inhabitants arrived in a trio of broken-down vehicles, and at least a dozen more came and went seemingly as the mood took them. There was lots of singing, carousing and a great deal of smoking, and their outlandish garb I can only describe as *most* peculiar - flared trousers, flower-pattern shirts and unbelievably garish colours. And that was just the men.

The strangest thing of all was their ingestion of some kind of *magical pill* - for it seemed that whenever they took it, they experienced a form of 'out-of-body experience' - I could see faint, veil-like versions of each of them, floating around the rooms in which their bodies sat.

It was at that point that some of them became aware of *me*, to a degree, and I remember the fearful anxiety that could suddenly overcome one or more of these 'pill-poppers'. As with the little girl who had moved in after I had passed away, I always did my best not to bother them when they were in that heightened state of agitation, and eventually their awareness of me would seemingly subside.

Over time, the commune began to reduce in number. So too did the length of the hair. Even the clothing became a little less silly; the times were changing, I suppose.

Eventually, from the original group only a man and a woman remained - who I noticed had got married one day when they returned to their house in wedding regalia. A daughter soon followed, who was lovely. Tom, Joanna and Jessica; three of my favourites, I think.

As time went on, I became aware of all the technological marvels happening in the world - there was a rapid increase in the number of motorcars on the roads outside, I had noticed, and I began to look in awe through the windows at all the giant aeroplanes in the sky. The same applied to the interior of the home; the radio and gramophone we used 'in our day' were replaced by ever-more-raucous versions of the same, and I can't begin to tell you my amazement at the 'cinema box' that seemed to become a necessity in almost every room. When I had died there was a new movie that had just come out, about a giant monkey in New York - I had always hoped to see it with my husband, and one day I drifted down to 'sofa level' when no-one was around as the 'cinema box' was actually showing it! If I could still cry, I would have done so then.

With this new family of three, I could genuinely *feel* the glow of contentment within the walls of the house. The girl grew to university-age and disappeared for a short time, but I was delighted to see she came home almost every weekend. Her campus must have been nearby, so she had the benefit of not having to move away.

Even more of a surprise was when a baby bump began to show on her, shortly after she'd finished university. There was never any hint of 'a father on the scene', but within the year there was a beautiful, healthy girl named Louisa in the household.

I come now to the most unsettling part of my tale; the arrival of Aunt Cynthia. She was a pencil-thin, *severe* looking woman; I can find no better description.

It was about eight years after the birth of Louisa. I recall watching the family's motorcar through a window early one evening as it ambled back to the house. I had a sense that something was *wrong* about the car; there was a peculiar black aura emanating from it, almost like smoke - but this smoke was coming from the *rear* of the vehicle, not the front (where I presumed engines still resided in this futuristic age). This black smoke seemed like the polar-opposite of my 'wispy white cloud' self. Quite bizarre.

When they got out, the family were quieter than usual, I noticed; they were hushed and almost *awkward* in their behaviour, as if trying to be on their best behaviour. Even young Louisa was silent - a highly unusual sight.

The reason for their reservation in the back seat; the stick-like Aunt Cynthia sat in the back, and, once Tom had opened the door for her, she slowly got out to look on the house disapprovingly.

As she stood there, I noticed the wispy black vapours swirling around her - she wasn't smoking; this was her 'aura', for want of a better word. And it was a very bad one.

It was clear from a trio of suitcases even older than myself that she was planning to stay for a while, so I indulged in a little eavesdropping. Aunt Cynthia, it transpired, was moving in - to 'assist' her relatives; whatever *that* entailed.

Her actions (and general disapproval toward everything, especially Tom) allowed me to work out fairly quickly the true meaning of this set of affairs - the family were having a hard time financially, and so she was here to help them out. It was clear she blamed Tom for this, as she was soon treating him no better than a lackey.

"If he can't support his own family, he can at least *work* for *me*," was her icy rationale, spat out at regular intervals when Tom was within earshot.

Joanna protested when Aunt Cynthia got especially poisonous, but she was always met with the same response; "Do you want my money or *not*, dear?"

A few days after Aunt Cynthia's arrival, a removals vehicle arrived with a houseful of her hideous furniture. Most of the family's 'comfortable, bohemian and eclectic' collection of interior items were transported by Tom to the garage, and Aunt Cynthia's ancient alternatives took over the house.

The slouchy sofa was replaced with a series of upright, high-backed chairs that looked frankly painful to sit on, while the family's framed pictures of popular film and music artists were discarded in favour of a series of Victorian-style cameos of obscure relatives even more dead than myself.

After this, poor Tom was set to work pasting up hideously drab wallpapers in every room, each more prehistoric than the last.

Within a month the house had been transformed from a comfortable family home into something only a shrivelled old twig like Aunt Cynthia would find tasteful; it felt more like a mausoleum.

I was pleased to see that young Louisa *despised* Aunt Cynthia. She would have as little to do with her as possible and began spending more time in my favourite room; the spare bedroom in the annexe.

As you may have guessed by now, Aunt Cynthia wasn't the kind of person who liked to be ignored, so on one Saturday afternoon, when Louisa had failed to respond to her calls from downstairs, she slowly made her way up to the bedroom, in order to say a word or two to the child about respecting her elders (and *betters*, she no doubt thought).

I think Aunt Cynthia had actually planned this little tête-à-tête with Louisa in advance; she'd told Joanna, Tom and Jessica to fetch provisions, and had offered to supervise Louisa in their absence.

I remember watching the poor girl's face as she heard the hard rap of Aunt Cynthia's shoes on the upstairs landing getting closer, and saw the sinister silhouette of her great-aunt standing at the entrance to the room.

Naturally, poor Louisa received the kind of withering lecture about 'respect' that spiteful, bitter old women unleash on innocent children when their mothers are out of earshot. And naturally she threatened the child with unspeakable evils should she ever go running to her mother or grandparents about what had been said. One of the threats involved sending the girl away; another involved locking her in the basement. If I'd have had the ability to fling myself at that harridan there and then I would have done so. I was just so utterly in awe at how that little girl held in her sobs as that poison was poured into her ears.

The noise of the car returning was the cue for Aunt Cynthia to 'allow' Louisa to leave, and the poor child couldn't exit that room fast enough.

I was shocked by what came next, however.

"And I think we're going to have to do something about *you*," Aunt Cynthia said to me, coldly staring up at the corner where I had been watching the proceedings unfurl.

Without another word, she turned and left the bedroom.

Several days later, the family (without Aunt Cynthia) left for what looked like a short vacation. Once they had driven away, she poured herself a small glass of sherry and walked to the living room. Sitting on a high-backed chair parked close to a telephone, she calmly dialled a number and had a brief conversation with someone. After it was ended, she waited, virtually unmoving. With a slight, inscrutable smile and eyes gently closed she sat throughout this wait, looking ever so much like an extremely smug Siamese cat.

An hour later, I heard the noise of a car pulling into the driveway in front of the house. After the doorbell rang, she quietly got up and answered the door.

The man who entered was as stick-thin and severe-looking as she was. An Irish priest, I noticed from his dress and accent - though whereas most Irish accents can be described as a brogue, this was most definitely a bark.

I listened in a little on their conversations, before suddenly feeling the need to retreat.

"... And you say you can actually *see* this abomination, Cynthia?" the priest snarled.

"Oh, yes, Father Cassidy," Cynthia replied, "it's watching us now - *aren't you*, dear?" Cynthia shot a look in my direction, and I couldn't help wanting to remove myself from their presence.

Voices followed me as I drifted away. "It tends to lurk in the child's playroom - the bedroom in the annexe."

"God in heaven - well, we can't have that."

"My feelings exactly, Father."

Before I knew it I was back in my 'favourite' corner in the annexe bedroom, with Cynthia and the priest staring up at me. I could tell from his vague squinting he had no awareness of me, but seemed to respect (or was that fear) Cynthia's word on the matter.

"Just do what's necessary, Father - then we can have a nice cup of tea."

Dressed all in black as per the priestly fashion, he began reading from a leather-bound Bible. Droning words in Latin quickly became a chant, spoken over and over. This *hurt me*, I soon discovered. I neither understood the words nor cared about them particularly - but they were calling to me, compelling me ... compelling me to *leave the house*!

This couldn't be. This oration, this *performance* and its effect on me seemed beyond reason. I looked beyond the priest and saw the hideous grin of satisfaction on Aunt Cynthia's face - and her black aura was reaching out shivering wispy tendrils as if in elation. I felt myself sliding against my will from my lofty position in the far corner of the bedroom, my vapour-like essence turning to a painful, oily slickness as I slowly slid further and further down the wall - and though I couldn't be seen by the priest I was suddenly aware he could *hear me* when I let out a pain-wracked scream.

The man in black staggered backward several steps in his shock, but girded himself anew to launch into a louder, more frenzied reading from his little book. In my desperation I launched myself forwards in an attempt to retrieve it from him, but was *burned* when I tried to do so; it was untouchable, and I screamed again.

The furniture within the room began to shake violently, as did the doors and windows. This was not my doing; I was unsure if this was some residual effect of the energies that I either unwillingly emit or surround me, but I could claim no ownership on these acts. The ceiling lamp blew out, leaving the three of us in a twilight darkness; only the street lights outside the bedroom window gave the room some scant illumination. The bedroom window rattled and shook and blew open, straining each frame on its hinges. And I was pushed at speed toward its opening.

Soon I was clinging on, the oily form I had become stretching itself across the window's orifice in a desperate last attempt to prevent myself from being hurled out. I did not know why I feared this, but something deep in my consciousness told me *I have to remain inside.*

I heard the priest roaring again; he bellowed his words and his stunted perceptions could finally make out at least part of the slick, oiled, pain-wracked shape I had become. Behind him I could see Aunt Cynthia sneering; I could feel her hatred toward me; she would have me *destroyed*, not understood.

I heard another voice. A tiny one. Two words over the melee; but the last of my resisting strength was spent and all faded to blackness.

At some point later that day, I became aware of Tom changing the lightbulb in the annexe bedroom. I looked around and could see Joanna holding the ladder for him, while Jessica sat playing with Louisa.

"She's awake," smiled the child to her mother, and then the strangest thing happened; all four of them looked up to me in my corner.

Tom came down from the ladder and tentatively walked toward me. "Erm, I hope you can hear us oka-."

"She *can*, grandfather," Louisa interrupted with a giggle, "and her name's Emmeline".

He continued, awkwardly. "Emmeline. Fine. Well, I'm not sure if you understood what happened, Emmeline, but I'm afraid Aunt Cynthia shooed us away on a trip and sneaked in that priest to try and get rid of you."

This took a little getting used to. People - living people - were aware of me; talking to me; engaging me in a conversation. A one-way conversation, I will admit, but one in which I was being acknowledged. And no-one was terrified.

"It was *Louisa* who knew what was going on," I heard Jessica saying. "Oh, and 'Hello', by the way." She waved in my direction and blushed, before continuing.

"The moment she knew Aunt Cynthia was on the phone to the priest, Louisa bawled and bawled in the car until we promised to turn around and come home. When we got back, she ran upstairs and shouted 'That's enough!' - and it broke the exorcism rite they'd concocted between them."

"It also knocked Aunt Cynthia and that priest clear off their feet," smirked Joanna, as she smiled down at her grandchild with more than a little pride.

I couldn't believe what I was hearing. There was more.

"Louisa's known about you all along," Joanna continued. "We've all had our *suspicions* about this room over the years, but she spotted you from the day she could see. She's *gifted*, to say the least. We're only just getting a grasp of what she can do, but it's quite wonderful. Oh, and she says you're cool, by the way."

Cool. Not a word from my day, but there's a first for everything, I suppose.

Joanna spoke again. "Anyhow, you don't need to worry about Aunt Cynthia anymore, Emmeline. We've packed that old witch off in a taxi back to where she came from, and the priest went scuttling close behind. Money or no money, she's too venomous to have around."

Joanna looked around at her family. "And guys, while I'm thinking on, I think tomorrow would be a good day to grab our gear back out of the garage."

And so that's my story. My story so far, at least - for who's to say now that my story cannot continue, even in death? Having found someone who perceives me and hears my thoughts without fear is something novel, delicious and quite exciting. This sweet, little, *gifted* Louisa and I have much to communicate about I'm sure, and I pray she has a long lifetime ahead of her to share with me.

For I am a ghost.

I am *the* ghost of 213 Peverill Road.

I inhabited this house when I was alive, and I continue to do so now.

And I have a family.

THE END

THE CREMATORIUM

At the top of the tallest hill in the ancient market town of Littlewych sits Littlewych Crematorium. At the top of Littlewych Crematorium sits a tall, cigar-shaped chimney from which smoke and ashes billow every Friday evening.

The locals of Littlewych make the kind of morbid jokes you might expect when they see these plumes of smoke. Some give a dark chuckle and check their watches, for the crematorium's proprietor was a man known for his time-keeping.

Whenever they would see the first wisps of smoke escaping from the chimney, they knew it has just turned 6pm. *"Frying tonight,"* the older children would cackle grimly. Others would debate amongst themselves as to who the smoke and ash might belong to; was it old Mrs Collington who died last week, or maybe that unfortunate couple from out of town in that nasty road accident the weekend before?

Eleanor Armitage, a dour, sour-faced woman (who unfortunately lived downwind of the prevalent south-westerly winds that blew in from the sea) would curse her luck for buying the house she lived in, and seal her doors and windows from the choking ash and smoky odour that wafted her way with the onset of every weekend. She paid a small fortune to the local window cleaner in her never ending battle against the ashen muck that built up on her windows, and vowed to never be cremated in Littlewych Crematorium.

Zacchariah Blake was the crematorium's proprietor. A burly, bearded, middle-aged man, he was a former soldier who had battled in many overseas military campaigns in his youth, and left parts of his body on foreign fields to show for it.

As a consequence of being a former soldier and now an undertaker, it would be fair to say he was the kind of man who could be said to be closer to God, and closer to the realm of death. Death didn't bother Zacchariah Blake - prior to taking on ownership of the crematorium, he had seen and experienced enough of it and all its associated horrors to ensure he always remained stoic, impassive and professional in his duties.

So it came as quite a surprise when, after thirteen continuous years of professional service within the undertaking business, he suddenly and quite abruptly cancelled all future bookings and diverted all his trade to the funeral directors in the nearby towns of Grantwych and Toehampton.

Being something of a closed, insular market town, the inhabitants of Littlewych naturally began to talk in earnest amongst themselves when the 6pm smoke failed to billow out of the crematorium's chimney on the following Friday. A cluster of 'concerned' (nosey) citizens traipsed up the hill to the crematorium the following Saturday morning, but were met with silence when they yanked on the iron bell-chain at the gates to the building.

Peering through the gates in an attempt to see movement

behind the crematorium's stained glass windows also proved fruitless, as did the great many calls to the crematorium's phone number.

It was a full month before anyone heard from Zacchariah Blake - and even then it was in an indirect, and rather curious manner.

He placed an advertisement in the Littlewych Times, which read thus;

Situations Vacant

Writer / interviewer / cameraperson / similar
required to record one night at Littlewych Crematorium

Must have strong mind and stomach

Payment: £2,000

Send your details via post to Littlewych Crematorium
Successful applicant will be contacted

Five weeks later, the successful applicant pulled on the iron bell-chain at the gates of Littlewych Crematorium. She had amassed quite an (unwanted) entourage around her, as virtually the entire town - with the exception of Eleanor Armitage - had traipsed up the hill to glean any and all information about this curious set of affairs.

She was bombarded with questions as she struggled up the hill with a backpack-load of equipment. Why did *she* get the job? Why was *she* so special? What sort of *young woman* wants to spend a night *in a crematorium*? Is she only doing it *for the money*?

Ava Sawyer had wondered these same questions herself, and didn't need a gaggle of rubbernecking townies throwing their queries at her with increasing frustration. She kept her eyes forward as she schlepped up the hill, focussing on the tall chimney stack until she reached the gates.

Once she'd rung the bell and heard the automatic 'clack' of the gate being opened, she squirreled inside - careful not to let any of the surrounding locals in as well, lest the shut gate become an open *floodgate*. Once she'd managed this and closed it behind her, the volume of the townsfolk on the other side of the gate rose and rose, until it almost sounded as if they were baying for her blood. *No*, she told herself, *sheep don't bay for blood* - just ignore them.

Ava crossed the courtyard to the main entrance, and stepped inside the door (which she noticed had been left open for her).

She looked around the entrance hallway; there was an empty reception desk and some chairs for guests. A photo was mounted on the wall with the name Zacchariah Blake engraved beneath it. It showed a burly, bearded, middle-aged man. Dark brown hair, a polite smile and a smart suit. A big, strong-looking fellah. Respectable.

Nothing like the man now standing at the far end of the entrance hallway.

This man was gaunt in appearance; *haggard*, even - his well-built physique reduced to a skeletal frame. Bearded, yes, but all notion of colour had gone from both his beard and his hair - which was now a shock of pure white.

"Ms. Sawyer," the man rasped weakly, "won't you come this way?"

"Mr Blake?" Ava asked uncertainly.

The man chuckled weakly in response, his weak, rheumy eyes passing from her to the photo. "I will admit my appearance has changed a little in the past few weeks," he replied, "and if you still wish to stay this evening, I'll show you *why*."

Zacchariah Blake invited Ava to follow him, and they went from the entrance area to a small chapel room. Although Littlewych Crematorium was, as its name suggested, a place where the deceased were merely cremated (as the majority of funeral services were conducted at places of worship elsewhere), the chapel was still there in case any relatives of the deceased needed it at short notice. In truth, it never got used, and Ava noticed how spotlessly clean it was.

She sat on a pew, while Mr Blake went off to make them both a drink. He returned a couple of minutes later, with a tray of coffee and biscuits.

"Mr Blake," she asked after taking a sip of coffee, "can you tell me why I was chosen for this assignment over the other candidates? From what I saw outside, there are many people who are intrigued by your advertisement in the local rag."

"You're right, there have been over a thousand applications," he answered, "and I doubt old Jerry the postman's been happy about lugging them all up this hill. But the truth is, *I* didn't choose you - my guest did."

"Your guest?" Ava raised an eyebrow. "I'd assumed we were alone in the crematorium."

Zacchariah Blake smiled ruefully. "We're not. And you'll meet my guest later." He also drank some coffee, and went silent for a short while as if in deep thought, before continuing. "Now, Ms. Sawyer - may I just check all is as agreed ..."

Ava nodded, shimmied off her sizeable backpack and laid-out the contents on to the pew beside her. She was glad to get it off her back; it was only after starting the hike up to Littlewych Crematorium that she'd realised she should have arranged for a cab.

It contained a mobile phone, an old style compact film camera with several reels of film and sound recording equipment, a telescopic tripod, a notepad and pen and a small tupperware tub of food for herself.

"It's all *analogue*, like you asked for," she advised, indicating toward the gear. "Used to belong to my dad back in the seventies, when he was a location filmer for the BBC. We checked it all, and it runs fine. Pretty durable, too - my father's been in both the Arctic and the Tropics with this set of kit."

Looking everything over, Mr Blake nodded in satisfaction. "Good; I don't want any *digital* recording equipment, like I'd mentioned. Digital recordings can be accused of being *tampered with*; straight onto film and tape is what we need for tonight. Keeps things genuine."

This insistence on old-school analogue gear had left Ava curious, but Zacchariah Blake was paying for it all, so she was happy to leave her questions unanswered for now.

He continued; "Once we've finished our drinks, you can leave the phone here - as we discussed, no phones allowed past this point. It'll be sitting here waiting for you in the morning. Oh, and the money will be sitting in your account at 9am tomorrow."

"All sounds good," Ava replied. "So, where did you want me to begin? Did you want me to film in here, then move on to the other rooms or-?"

Mr Blake smiled weakly. "Oh no, it's not quite like that. We'll be in *one room only* tonight - near the furnace and the freezers. I'll take you there and you can get set up. I'll explain more once we're there."

"I call this *the workroom*," Mr Blake said, as he ushered Ava inside. It was a large open space at the rear of the chapel; at the opposite end was a curved brick wall, streaked with carbon-marks rising upwards to the ceiling from an immense iron door set in its centre. Ava realised this was the furnace before Mr Blake explained as much. In the middle of the room sat three enormous slab-like mortuary tables - each the length of a human body, and then some. There was a wall of inset cupboards, in which she assumed he kept various 'undertaking equipment' - embalming fluid and the like, if her memory of gothic horror films was anything to go by.

What made her shudder was the opposite wall. Here were the square, unmistakable doors of the 'mortuary freezers' - which her knowledge of cop shows told her was where all 'the stiffs' were kept.

"I'll get the fire going," Mr Blake said, indicating toward

the furnace. "We'll need it later, when it gets cold."

Ava shrugged, as she started to unload and assemble her gear. It wasn't a chilly evening by any means, though she admitted they were pretty exposed up on the top of the hill.

She heard the 'whumpf' of the furnace's flames being ignited, and stopped for a moment to see the orange glow fill the tiny window of the furnace door.

Mr Blake pointed to a corner. "I'd recommend positioning your camera over there," he gestured. "You'll be able to get the whole room in shot then." He then pointed to the mortuary slabs. "And make the slabs the focal point - most of the filming will probably happen there."

Ava did as asked, and spent a short while loading up film and checking sound quality, while Mr Blake wandered off to check on the 'rabble' outside.

He looked so *resigned*, thought Ava, as he shuffled away - as if something bad has happened to him and he's powerless to do anything about it. What could it be? Illness? A cancer? He certainly looked ill enough.

"I see most of them have gone," he said on his return. "I'm sure you won't be bothered when you leave tomorrow."

"Well, I'm just about set up," said Ava. "I'm guessing this is going to be an interview of some kind. Did you want to fill me in on details, or-."

"Let's just say it'll be *my guest* that does the talking," he replied, interrupting her.

"Not *yourself*, then?" she queried.

Mr Blake looked at his watch. "Well … it'll be a while before my guest's up and about, so you can 'warm up' with interviewing me, if you wish."

Once the camera was running and Mr Blake was in position, Ava began with the only question that sprang to mind; "So, please tell me about yourself, Mr Blake."

This he proceeded to do. Though visibly weak, Zacchariah Blake took his time and gave a lengthy account of much of his life. It was almost as if the telling was some form of cathartic unburdening for him - and he looked more relieved with every sentence he spoke.

He skimmed over his childhood, which he felt was both 'grim and pointless', and quickly moved on to his time in the military. At first he gave a resumé of the places he'd been stationed at, and talked about some of the more colourful characters he'd served with - and even laughed a little in recollection of some of the humourous moments he and his squad had managed to grasp out of some decidedly 'hairy' situations.

He talked about his wounds, proudly showing them to the camera; Ava was surprised to discover that much of his left leg was prosthetic, though he walked without a limp even in this new, emaciated version of himself. It had been lost to a landmine in Xanbaru whilst he was part of a UN peacekeeping force there, he explained.

Halfway through, Mr Blake broke off and unearthed a bottle of whiskey and two glasses from a cupboard - it appeared the reminiscences were making him a little nostalgic.

All in all, he spent about an hour in front of the camera, talking in a frail but jovial manner about his army days. However, whether it be down to the whiskey or just the need to get it off his chest - the tone became more ominous as he shifted to more darker themes.

"Of course, it wasn't all about clearing out insurgents and helping the locals build better lives," he began. "I've seen some truly awful things. Innocent families killed; the children are the worst. Oh, the things I could describe to you. And not all from the opposing side; we made mistakes, sometimes. And sometimes we knew *exactly* what we were doing. We'd put away the rule book out of a need for *sheer bloody revenge.* We were only human. You'd get a crazy bastard in our squad who just wanted to take it out on the next man, woman or child they saw - because their best mate got blown up by a kid in a suicide vest that morning - and ... well, you find it hard not to go along with it."

"And then you'd get the *crazy stuff* happening," he continued. "The stuff that just didn't make sense. You'd be standing over the corpse of a dead kid one day, and then *he'd* be *standing there* the next night, *staring at you* at the end of your camp bed, white as a sheet. I have *seen* toothless old hags that had their brains blown out grinning at me night after night after night. Dead mates up and walking the barricades the night after they'd been filleted by some insurgent the day before. The doctors would put it down to PTSD and everything else, but there was more to it than that. I wasn't seeing things. Me and death - we've always been close. We'd be stuck in some Godless hole in the middle of a desert somewhere, doing things no man should be asked to do for no justifiable reason, and you just felt like hell was laughing at you."

Ava shivered. She was getting cold after all, and it wasn't just the harrowing stories from Mr Blake.

He was shivering too, which seemed to prompt him to

look at his watch; "Anyway, enough about me. You should get ready for my guest, Ms. Sawyer - stick another roll of film in, or whatever - he'll be ready any minute."

Ava noticed the room temperature decidedly *plummet* as she added another reel to the camera. Soon she had 'dragon breath' and wished she'd fetched a scarf and gloves. Hoar frost began to form on the steel doors of the freezers, and was rapidly creeping vine-like toward the other walls. She had to pull her sweater's arms over her fingers, to stop her skin sticking to the camera metal as she busily completed her work.

"Are your freezers on the blink?" she grumbled to Mr Blake, as she shuddered from the sudden cold, "it should be *like a furnace* in here from your ... y'know, furnace."

"They're working fine," he replied quietly. "Now, if we're all set and running again, I suggest you come over to where it's warmer."

"But I'll be in shot, then," she replied.

"Exactly. I need you to talk to my guest in front of the camera, Ms. Sawyer."

"Just *who is* your guest, Mr-."

Ava was cut short by a tremendous *clang* on one of the refrigerator doors. She elicited a scream, and turned her head to see who had made it.

There was no-one there.

The bang slowly faded, til all that could be heard was the gentle rumble of the gas pipes that powered the furnace.

"Is this some kind of *sick prank*, Mr Blake?" Ava barked. "Some wind-up for your army mates, that you wanted on film for everyone to laugh at?"

Mr Blake was solemn and unmoving. He look *sorrowful*, even. "No prank, I can assure you."

"Then wh-." Again, Ava was cut short.

And again, there was a tremendous clang on one of the refrigerator doors.

Mr Blake's sad, watery eyes slowly looked over at the third door. "*The dead* would talk with you, Ms. Sawyer."

He then moved slowly to the third refrigerator door, and began to force open the latch.

"No!" replied Ava, perhaps instinctively, and reached out to stop him. But it was too late.

With a hiss of air pressure and a foul stench that almost knocked Ava from her feet, the door was pushed open.

Swirling mist and darkness. That was all Ava could see within the open refrigerator.

And then the green glow of two staring eyes.

She gasped as she fell back; first against Mr Blake and then against one of the mortuary tables.

The eyes moved closer; the figure inside was *crawling* out of the refrigerator. A moment later Ava screamed again, when the room's light fell upon the figure's face.

The crawling figure was barely whole; little more than a skeleton with slivers of flesh hanging limply from its bones. Its baleful eyes floated within their sockets, its gumless teeth a reaper's smile. A sickening rattle came from what remained of its throat.

Slowly, carefully - like a spider exiting a hole - the figure crept out of the refrigerator, its lidless eyes on Ava the whole time. It scuttled toward her suddenly in an entirely inhuman manner, causing her to scream again.

Over the noise of her pounding heart, Ava heard Mr Blake speaking. "You're quite safe, Ms. Sawyer, I assure you. It's only *fascinated*. You have so much life."

She looked at him in desperation, as she tried to inch around the mortuary slab away from this *thing*.

"*Must have strong mind and stomach*," Mr Blake said. "Remember the advertisement?"

"W-why ... why me?" she stammered in response. "What do you want *me* for?"

"To ssssspread my messssage," the creature hissed in return, which made Ava shriek. It was closer now, easily within grasping distance of her, yet made no move toward her.

"M-message?" she found herself querying, trying desperately not to retch from the nauseating stench coming from its oozing mouth.

"Yeeeesssssss," it responded, "I would have the world know *the truth* of the other sssssiiiiiiide."

"Who ... *a-are* you?" Ava asked, wincing from its breath.

The creature retreated a little, perhaps conscious its close proximity was causing Ava such distress, and gestured to Mr Blake to speak on its behalf.

"The body is the corpse of Roald Sigurdsson, who died about six or seven weeks ago," said Mr Blake. "The thing inhabiting Mr Sigurdsson's corpse is, well, shall we say, *not* Mr Sigurdsson. I was performing my funeral duties in the usual way when it made itself known to me. You could say it has kept me here ever since - and has drained me of my life in order to survive, as you can see."

Ava was looking at the door to the workroom, to flee, but

Mr Blake thought it best to advise against it.

"I'm afraid we're trapped, you and I. The cold it emits will have sealed the door shut and you'd only rip the flesh from your hands if you touched the door handle. But you *are* quite safe; an arrangement has been made to secure your passage, and it seems to honour deals - a bit like Satan, I suppose. Anyway, you *will* leave here in the morning; I've been assured."

Mr Blake stopped as he realised something. "Is the camera still running? Are we capturing all this?"

Ava nodded weakly, tears welling in her eyes.

"Goooooood," the creature answered in its loathsome hiss, "then I wwwill beginnn."

"I ammm here to ssshow your world the trrruth of the other sssiiiide. Your notionssss of heaven are a liiie; there is nooo paradissssse. There is only the dark, and the thingsss that dwell within the darrrrrk. The thhhhiiiings that wwwill prey on youuuu in the darrrk. The things that willlll hound you, and caaaaatch you, and tear yourrrr sssssoul to piecessss, foreverrrr and foreverr once you aaaare dead. Rrregardlesssss of whether you have lived a gooooood liiife, or a baaad life, we are waaaiting for youuuuu. There issss noo esssscape."

The creature spoke on in this manner for some time, until it had decided its message had been delivered. "Avaaaa Sssawyerrr, I have tassssked you to take this mmmessssage to the wwworld. If you doooo thisss, yourrr fate in the afterlife willl be lesssss severrrre."

"W-why tell the world all this?" she asked in response. "Why do people need to know?"

"Thhheeeey live a falsse life of hope wiiithout feearrr," it responded, "and I *waaaannt* theiirrr feearrrr. It is beeetttter they know the truuuth of deathh; of what issss waiting for themmm. That *I* am waiting for themmm. I wanttt to be the last thing theyyy think of wwwwhen they die, forrr I wiiiill be eeeverything they sssssseeee for eternityyy. And there issss no escape from meeeee."

It looked toward Mr Blake. "Now; the arraaangemeeent, Miiisssster Blake."

Mr Blake nodded slowly, and walked toward the furnace. He heaved on the iron door and pulled it open. There was a sudden rush of heat as the door swung back against the wall.

"My life for yours," he called to Ava, "and the crematorium now belongs to you. Enjoy your days, while you can."

Zacchariah Blake then proceeded to climb inside, groaning and then screaming as his hands and knees began to smoke and catch fire as he crawled further and further inside. After a few seconds his body slumped to one side of the furnace entrance and the rest of his body was engulfed in flame.

Sobbing and shaking in disbelief, Ava looked back at the creature she shared the room with.

"Until neeext tiiimme," it rasped, before it followed Mr Blake's steps to the furnace and crawled inside.

THE END

... EXIT

"**W**hat a *ridiculous* collection of stories," Quentin D'Orsey snorted derisively. "It's all utter *tommyrot*, Mr Charon, and it's also rather discourteous of you to reel out that kind of morbid claptrap to your guests." The others in the room noticed that, despite Mr D'Orsey's brusque, arrogant manner, he was actually shaking like a leaf.

"Are you saying your story is *untrue*, Mr D'Orsey?" Ms Jaya Balakrishnan asked.

He gave no answer. After a time, she spoke again. "Well, I can confirm to you all, now that the events have all been replayed to me, that my story is correct. I was trapped in that flying 'tin can' for a month with that ... *monster*."

Captain Jeddoe nodded in agreement. Like D'Orsey, he was shaking also. "I go by all that has been said this evening ... if *evening* this be. Before this lonely place I had no recollection - but now my memory is clear."

Mrs Digby spoke next, to Mr Charon. "You're telling us that we're all ... dead. Somehow I knew, but I wasn't ..." She tailed off.

"Yes," said Mr Blake solemnly, "that's exactly what he's telling us."

"Well, in that case, I shouldn't *be* here," exclaimed Travis, "and you can send me back. I mean - *I survived*, didn't I? Mary and I escaped from the fire in the theatre, and we got away. You all heard that."

Mr Charon shrugged apologetically. "Alas, I neglected to mention that you were killed *a week later*, Mr Benton. All that horrendous rain you were having loosened those overflowing drainpipes at your residence, and one fell down and knocked you on the head whilst you were on your doorstep."

Travis sunk back into his seat, a look of defeat on his face.

"And what of me?" exclaimed Yatima, defiantly. "I did not die!"

"Well, the *human* part of you did," Mr Charon reasoned. "I'm afraid the eight-legged *thing* that's now scuttling around your village at night certainly can't be classed as human."

Mr Charon clapped his hands. "Anyhow! Stuff to do and places to be. Ladies and gentlemen, if you'll kindly follow me I'll take you to your final destination."

Collecting up their glasses and tossing them unceremoniously behind the cocktail bar, Mr Charon extended a hand to guide them through a pair of large doors identical to the ones through which they'd entered.

These opened into a dark cavern of sorts, illuminated here and there by the occasional swinging lantern. The guests could hear the creaking of timbers under their feet as they walked, along with the sloshing of water; looking down, they realised they were now standing on a wooden jetty.

Tethered to a post was a long boat; it had the capacity to hold about eight passengers and was not dissimilar in its slimline dimensions and appearance to an Italian gondola.

Whispering a jaunty little tune to himself, Mr Charon

bade them to take a seat on the boat, and when all were carefully aboard he cast off.

He took to the rear of the vessel - masterfully standing on its aft timbers like a Venetian gondolier - and began to propel the craft slowly forward through the black waters by means of a long barge pole.

Soon the last of the lantern lights had faded from view and the party found themselves gently travelling in utter darkness, with the splash and splosh of Mr Charon's barge pole the only sound.

There was so much about all that had transpired that made no sense to the passengers; their lack of recollection about their lives prior to their meeting on the misty landscape, and the strange waiting room in the middle of nowhere. The bizarre stories about themselves and each of their companions, and their easy resignations in accepting the truth of each tale.

And why was the charming Mr Charon devoid of all skin and flesh - no more than a *living skeleton in a suit*?

These seven lost souls would perhaps never know.

THE END

OTHER BOOKS AVAILABLE:

The Complete Murkmyre Saga

The Idiot

Out of my Head

Ísklo - A Dragon Tale

Augustus, the Hairy Zummabeest

The Slug that Saved Christmas

The Easter Bunny Invasion

The Easter Bunny's Outer Space Adventure

The Easter Bunny's Undersea Adventure

Utterly Bonkers (with Phoenix Petit-Hayes)

Grandma Grunt

Grandad's Bottom

Horrid Horatia

Hairy Tales

Verity Fruitt and My Magic Gonk

For other titles available (printed, ebook and audiobook formats), do a search for 'Clifford James Hayes' on Amazon.

www.ingramcontent.com/pod-product-compliance
Lightning Source LLC
Chambersburg PA
CBHW051451050726
47593CB00005B/2016